U0165701

B2B 作業研發篇

企業英語會話

Speak like a true B2B professional

李純白・著

五南圖書出版公司 印行

Preface 推薦序1

這本書教您用最簡單的英語跟國外客戶談生意，也教您用最文雅的英語跟國外的供應商殺價。

用英語跟國外客戶談生意，其實是大部分上班族學英語的終極目標。因為許多上班族努力學英語，目的就是想要找一份薪水比較高的工作，而企業之所以願意花高薪聘請英語比較好的員工，目的就是希望員工能直接用英語跟外國人談生意。

然而，許多的上班族雖然對自身的業務十分熟悉，也學過許多年的英語，但是在面對國外客戶或是供應商的時候說不出話來。舉例來說，所有的業務人員都知道報價有多麼的重要，但是卻有許多業務人員不知道「報價」的英語怎麼說？而就算知道了，也往往不知道要怎麼很自然地、主動地向客戶提起報價的事情。

再舉個例子來說，所有的採購人員都知道殺價的重要性，但是許多亞洲的採購人員面對國外供應商的時候，卻會吞吞吐吐的說不出話來。因為我們以前在學校學的都是客客氣氣的英語，開口閉口都是「請」、「謝謝」、「對不起」，但是我們在面對國外供應商的時候，總不能這樣溫良恭儉讓吧？

目前市面上的商業英語書籍，大多是由英語老師所編寫的，文辭雖然優美，但往往不切實際，一件簡單的事情說的翻來覆去的，卻說不到重點；教材中教了很多複雜的文法句型跟新字彙，但是卻沒有涵蓋國際商務上最常用的一些術語。

李純白老師是我在臺大棒球隊的學長，他從臺大商學系畢業之後，遠赴美國德拉瓦大學取得MBA學位，學有專精，英語非常好，又曾經在跨國公司工作過二十幾年，累積了非常豐富的國際貿易與跨國管理經驗。他寫的這個系列，就是一套專為亞洲人設計的商業英語教材，這套教材避開了艱深難懂的文法句型、不用偏僻冷門的字彙，教您在短時間之內，用最簡單但也最實用英語跟國外的客戶談生意、用最文雅但是強硬的英語跟國外供應商殺價。

這個系列原先是以線上教材的形式推出的，結合了我們公司的 MyET 英語學習平臺，讓學生們可以藉由聽跟說的方式，迅速地掌握商業英語的核心能力。而由於這套教材非常的實用，因此在短短的一年之間，已經有十幾家臺灣、中國大陸，以及日本的大學及企業集體採購使用。而這些企業及大學，也一再跟我們反應，希望能有一套相對應的紙本書籍，對教材中的字彙文法做更詳細的解釋、對各種句型的使用時機做更深入的說明。

這是一套內行人為專業的商務人士所寫的英語教材，相信您一定會喜歡。

林宜敬

艾爾科技股份有限公司執行長

Preface 推薦序2

在世界地球村的今日，跨國的貿易和商業往來也日益頻繁，對商業大學的同學而言，掌握和駕馭商業交易的英語會話實在非常重要。感謝李純白老師能編寫此一本實用的好書，同學們如能好好研讀，當可大幅提升自己的商用英文的程度。

張瑞雄

國立臺北商業大學校長

2014年8月

Preface 推薦序3

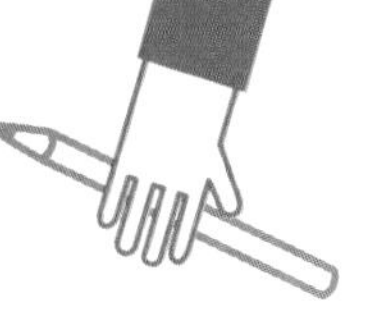

Being successful in building profitable and long term B2B relationships depends on building trust, and this does not happen overnight – it takes a diligent, thorough and professional approach, underpinned by a whole lot of hard work.

想要成功建立長期又能獲利的 B2B 買賣關係，勢必得由建立互信開始。然而 B2B 互信絕非一蹴可幾，得依靠一套結合勤奮不息、周密思考、與高度專業素養為一體的工作方法。

This exact approach was so powerfully demonstrated to me when I first started working with Paul, at a time when he was being challenged with the need to build brand value in the highly competitive Taiwan market. The approach worked, and Paul earned the trust and the respect of the customers and the suppliers.

當我初開始和 Paul 共事時，就強烈感受到這種工作方法的動力。當時，Paul 接下在高度競爭的台灣市場中，建立世界級品牌價值的挑戰。幾年下來，這套方法果真奏效，Paul 贏得客戶與供應廠商共同的尊敬與信任。

Communication between West and East is not as easy as may often be assumed these days – there are many cases where

misunderstandings have led to missed opportunities – damaging that trust that is so hard to build. This has not happened in the markets handled by Paul, and again it is fitting that his careful approach is explained in these books for the benefit of others. After all, there is nothing to be gained by re-inventing the wheel, and we can all learn from the experiences of others.

如今東西方之間的溝通並不如我們想像那般容易，一個小小誤解往往就導致喪失大商機。更糟糕的是，還可能危害到辛苦建立起來的互信。然而在Paul所負責的市場裡都未曾發生過這種情況。在這一套書裡，Paul 也詳細說明了上述的工作方法，希望能帶給他人更直接的利益。畢竟很多事情不需非得自行鑽研，我們隨時能夠從別人經驗中吸取到寶貴的現成方法。

In a typically practical manner, this series of books delivers guidance that is based on real life situations and current day conditions. It is entirely logical that students of his work therefore have the opportunity to benefit from his vast array of experience and wisdom, gained at the "coal face"; the "front line"; the "sharp end" through learning and using English.

在這一套書中，Paul 以一種專業又實用的著作方式，依據各種實際的經歷，配合當今的情況，提供專業意見給使用者參考。如此一來，我相信使用這套書的讀者，能從Paul親身在第一線作戰所累積的黑手實務經驗與企業智慧，透過英語的練習，獲得各種企業專業技能。

Andy Royal
Managing Director
Aero Sense Technologies
http://www.aerosensetech.com/index.html

Preface 作者序

我自幼就對英文有興趣。最早的記憶是學齡前總愛在空白紙上胡亂塗鴉些誰也看不懂的連體字形，母親因此來問我在寫些甚麼？我回應說：英文字啊！因為當時母親在聽廣播自學英文，家裡總能找到英文教材。耳濡目染之下，喜歡學習英文的興趣不知不覺陪我走過半個世紀。

成長於戰後時期，很自然的在上了初中（北市仁愛初中）之後，才開始接觸正規英文教育。初中有幸受教於三位十分出色的英文老師，讓我打下扎實的基礎。高中（北市成功中學）兩位英文老師，更用另類教法延續了我學習英語的熱情。而大一（台灣大學）遇見周樹華老師，則讓我見識到年輕優秀英文老師的實力和魅力。英文之所以能一路陪伴、協助我走過人生最精采的35年，實在要感謝這些良師們的引領及教導。

開心順手（口）使用英文是一回事，會想動手寫英語學習的書，又是另一回事，這全是機緣。2012年中偶然在閒聊之間，和學弟林宜敬（艾爾科技創辦人）有了合作開發自學英語數位教材的想法。藉由這機緣，讓我能將35年 B2B 職涯的專業與經驗，結合我的興趣，轉換成一套適合當今企業內部英語訓練使用的教材，短短半年間，完成了 MyET 的 MBA English 教材編寫。在數位教材上市後，進一步增加內容深度與廣度，完成了這套印刷版 B2B 企業英語訓練教材。擴編的

內容讓我能更貼近產業現狀，利用英語對話方式呈現企業內各部門對外溝通的情境，幫助使用者學到更實用的會話與寫作。

本系列書籍內容分成三本，分別是業務（Sales）、行銷（Marketing）、與作業研發（Operations and R&D）。這幾大部門，也是國內製造業裡，最經常使用英文對外聯繫的單位。內容編寫方式，是依據這四大部門對內對外的運作流程（業務），或者針對特定議題及情境（行銷與作業研發），以會話為主軸，輔以字彙、文法、及句型的解釋與示範。希望能利用工作的相似性，引起使用者的共鳴，自然的反覆練習，進而融會貫通並靈活運用在自身的工作上。

學習語言絕無捷徑，選對方法事半功倍。希望藉由貼近產業實務的編寫方式，讓英語學習變得更輕鬆、更自在。

特別感謝雙親，岳父母和家人的支持，尤其是在美國工作的女兒提供許多寶貴建議。感謝遠在英國的好同事 Andy Royal 專業指正，好友陳少君（Paul Chen）、蕭行志、艾爾科技林宜敬、屏東大學施百俊老師以及五南出版編輯團隊的協助。

李純白

Contents 目錄

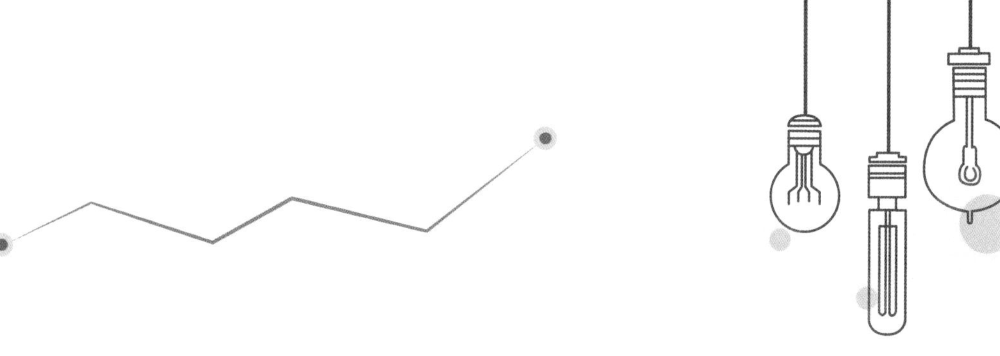

生產計劃

Production Planning

Summary 1

Production lead time has always been one of the most powerful strategic weapons for many manufacturers, particularly in the consumer electronics industry, semiconductor industry, and the components industry. Among many things deciding lead time, capacity planning and production planning are being dealt with on a daily basis and are having direct impacts on the competitiveness of the business. Nowadays, multi-plant-at-multi-place operations have become an industry trend. It is a difficult task for the operations department to optimize the capacity utilization rate on one hand and maintain a flexible production scheduling on the other. As a result, we constantly see communications and negotiations between sales and planning departments to achieve the revised delivery lead time required by the customers. Companies tend to gain competitiveness by maintaining maximum flexibility in the planning mechanism.

長久以來，縮短生產週期一直是生產型企業重要競爭策略之一，尤其現今消費性電子產業、半導體產業、以及相關零組件產業更是如此。在諸多影響生產週期因素中，產能規劃和生產計劃（生管排程）不但是企業每日都得緊盯的工作，更是直接影響整體競爭力最重要的企業功能。就日常生產作業來看，亞洲地區常見的多地多廠形態裡，經由產能最適化提高產能使用率，一直是作業部門最大挑戰。另一方面，生管還得隨時應付業務單位提出調整交期（提前或延後）的要求。因此不時可見雙方針對交期進行溝通、協調、與妥協。企業是否藉由維持彈性調度而形成競爭優勢，就愈發顯得重要。

生管排程：提前交貨 keep them happy

Eric: **Buyer, Baxton Computer (Singapore)** 採購

Alice: **Sales Rep, Ultimate Cleaning (Taiwan)** 業務代表

Phone conversation 電話交談

Eric: Alice, how soon can you ship the goods under our P.O. No.TS-120090-0630? I'm sorry to push you as I haven't received the O.A. from you.

Alice，我們 No.TS-120090-0630 那張訂單，你多久能出貨？很抱歉來催你，因為我還沒收到 O.A.。

Alice: No problem. For your reference, our standard lead time is four weeks after receiving the P.O. and we just confirmed a 21-day lead time by our O.A. BP605933.

沒關係。給你作參考，我們標準交期是收到訂單後四週。我們剛剛確認了 21 天交期，O.A. 號碼 BP605933。

Eric: So it's three weeks. I'm afraid we can't wait that long. We need the goods in two weeks.

那是三週啊！恐怕沒法等那麼久，我們得在二週內收到貨。

Alice: I'm sorry to hear that. I'll check with our factory and get back to you as quickly as I can.

真是抱歉。我現在立刻和工廠確認一下，會儘快回覆你。

Eric: Thanks very much, I will stay on the line while you check.

多謝了，我不掛斷，會在線上等你。

Alice：Good news, Eric! We'll be able to make it in two weeks.
好消息，Eric，我們能在二週內出貨。

Eric：Oh, that's great! I'm so relieved now.
太好了。現在我總算能鬆口氣了。

Alice：Good, thanks for your business and patience.
嗯，謝謝你的訂單和耐心。

Eric：Thanks again for your efforts.
再次感謝你的幫忙。

NOTE

❶**production lead time**：生產週期、生產前置期

指生產廠商從接單、備料、到出貨之間所需的時間，廣義等同交期。

Andy, our average production lead time, 3 to 5 weeks, is fairly competitive comparing to that of most competitors.

Andy，我們平均 3 至 5 週的交期，比起多數同行廠商算是很具競爭力了。

❷**powerful**：強大的、有力的

Daxconn has been so powerful in terms of capacity, manufacturing technology, and purchasing.

Daxconn 長久以來在產能、製造技術、以及採購能力上實力超強。

NOTE

❸ **strategic**：策略性的

James, one of our strategic competitive advantages is the nearly unlimited manufacturing capacity of our four huge plants in China.

James，我們策略競爭優勢之一，就是在中國境內四座超大規模工廠所能提供幾乎無上限的產能。

❹ **consumer electronics**：消費性電子產品

Dustin, consumer electronics such as digital cameras and video game consoles are the mainstays of our Suzhou plant.

Dustin，消費性電子產品如數位相機和遊戲主機，是我們蘇州廠的主力產品。

❺ **component**：零組件

❻ **among**：之中

通常用於三者或三者以上。

Linda, among so many component suppliers, Uni Steel is a very unique one.

Linda，在衆多零組件供應廠商之中，Uni Steel 很獨特。

❼ **capacity planning**：產能規劃

Marty, capacity planning is extremely important to us because we have five plants in three countries manufacturing different types of crystal oscillators.

Marty，產能規劃對我們來說極端重要，因為我們在三個國家共五座生產廠，分別生產不同種類的石英震盪器。

NOTE

❽ **production planning**：生產計劃，又稱生管

Mr. Suzuki, our production planning takes care of all the production scheduling of our 10 production lines. We are doing everything possible to pull in your orders as you requested.

Suzuki 先生，我們生管得負責廠內十條生產線的排程，我們正極盡可能依照你所要求幫你提前了。

註：pull in 提前交貨。

❾ **being dealt with**：處理、處置、應付（被動式）

Ricky, your request to pull in all outstanding orders is being dealt with by our planner.

Ricky，我們生管正在處理你提出全面提前出貨的要求。

註：outstanding orders 尚未完成出貨的訂單。

❿ **on a daily basis**：按每天（做某事）

Benny, being a junior in sales, you'd better spend some time working with the planners on a daily basis.

Benny，由於你業務資歷尚淺，最好每天能花些時間和生管一起共事。

⓫ **impact**：（名）衝擊、影響

Kevin, an order shortfall will definitely have a great impact on our capacity utilization rate and profitability as well.

Kevin，訂單不足必定嚴重衝擊我們產能使用率和獲利率。

註：shortfall 短缺、短少。

⑫ **nowadays**：現今、當今

Denise, nowadays, the production planning job is done online with the help of modern ERP systems.

Denise，現今生管排程工作都是藉由較先進的 ERP 系統在線上完成。

註：Denise 發音為 (KK)də`nis 或 (KK)də`niz。

⑬ **multi-plant-at-multi-place operations**：多地多廠營運

Mr. Wise, most Taiwan EMS firms are running the so-called multi-plant-at-multi-place operations in different Asian countries.

Wise 先生，多數台灣 EMS 廠家會在不同亞洲國家內，以多地多廠營運模式運作。

⑭ **task**：工作、任務、使命

Guys, the boss just gave us a tough task to find out TYC's capacity for TCXOs at their Xiamen plant.

各位，老闆剛剛給了一份苦差事，我們得查出 TYC 廈門廠 TCXO 的產能。

⑮ **optimize**：最優化、最適化

Eddie, don't you know that it is very difficult, if not impossible, to optimize the whole production operation as certain things always contradict each other?

Eddie，難道你不知道，由於總有一些事情相衝突，要將整個生產系統最優化，即便可能，也是極端困難嗎？

NOTE

⑯ capacity utilization rate：產能使用率

Sandy, what's happening to our capacity utilization rate as of now? You must be kidding me, because it reads 83%.

Sandy，我們現在的產能使用率是怎麼一回事？數字顯示才83%，你是在開我玩笑吧？。

⑰ on one hand…on the other：一方面…另一方面

Fiona, we're having a big problem now as we're being asked by sales to shorten the lead time by 3 weeks on one hand while the boss was asking us to achieve a 99% utilization target on the other.

Fiona，現在我們問題大了。一方面業務要求我們交期得縮短三星期，另一方面大老闆又要求達成 99% 使用率目標。

⑱ flexible：靈活的、有彈性的

Jason, the biggest problem we have concerning delivery is the lack of a flexible scheduling mechanism.

Jason，關於交期，我們最大的問題，在於缺乏一套靈活有彈性的排程機制。

⑲ as a result：因此

The system went down early in the morning. As a result, we did the scheduling manually.

今早系統當機，因此排程全用人工作業。

⑳ constantly：經常地、持續地

Adam, our production lines are constantly under tremendous pressure as a result of the ever-increasing orders.

Adam，由於訂單持續不斷成長，我們生產線的壓力好大。

㉑ communication：溝通

Justine, to work in the planning department, you must be able to handle tons of communications at any time.

Justine，要在生管部門做事，你得有辦法隨時從事大量的溝通工作。

㉒ negotiation：協商、交涉

Jeremy, it takes a great deal of emotional intelligence from all of the parties involved in any negotiation.

Jeremy，任何協商都需要每一參與者發揮高度情緒智慧。

㉓ revise：修正、改正

Mandy, the boss asked us to send him the revised version of the utilization forecast report no later than 3:00 p.m..

Mandy，老闆要我們在今天下午 3:00 以前，將修正過後的使用率預測報告傳給他。

㉔ tend to：傾向於、常常

Regarding delivery lead time, our customers tend to be asking a lot more flexibility from us.

關於交期，我們客戶常常要求更多的彈性空間。

NOTE

㉕ gain：獲得、贏得

Brian, I'm so happy to know we have successfully gained Baxton's full confidence in our capacity.

Brian，很開心知道我們已經成功贏得 Baxton 對我們產能的十足信心。

㉖ competitiveness：競爭力

Sandra, please bear in mind that our ample manufacturing capacity gives us a competitiveness that other companies will find difficult to match.

Sandra，請記住，我們充足的產能讓我們擁有一項其它公司難以匹敵的競爭力。

㉗ maximum flexibility：最大的彈性

Kevin, by keeping maximum flexibility in scheduling, we'll be able to accommodate any number of orders.

Kevin，藉由保持最大的彈性，我們將有辦法接下任何數量的訂單。

㉘ under our P.O. No.xxx：訂單編號xxx裡的貨，介系詞用 under。

㉙ push：催促、施壓

Joe, I don't mean to push you but you'd better respond more quickly to our pull-in request.

Joe，我沒有要催你，不過你得快點回覆我們提前出貨的要求。

㉚ O.A.：訂單確認

Order Acknowledgment 的縮寫，也可用 OACK 代表。

㉛ for your reference：提供你參考。

Just for your reference Ricky, we outperformed the March target by 20%.

Ricky，給你作參考：我們三月業績超標 20%。

㉜ confirm：確認、證實

Carl, our planner just confirmed that we'll be able to pull in all your outstanding orders by 5 days.

Carl，剛剛我們生管確認，有辦法將你們所有的未出貨訂單提前 5 天交貨。

㉝ I'm afraid：恐怕、抱歉

Joan, I'm afraid we won't be able to help you this time as we just don't have enough capacity.

Joan，由於我們產能不足，這次恐怕沒法幫你們忙了。

㉞ that long：那麼久

Our customers are pushing us real hard, we can't wait that long.

客戶催得緊，我們沒法等那麼久。

㉟ check with：與…核對、求證

Anna, please check with Cosmos Automation if they can accept our 3-week lead time.

Anna，請和 Cosmos Automation 求證看看，是否能接受我們三週的交期。

NOTE

㊱make it：做到、達成、完成

Phil, we'll make it if the materials arrive in time.

Phil，如果物料及時趕到，我們會來得及完成的。

㊲I'm so relieved：我大大鬆口氣

John, I'm so relieved that we'll have enough capacity by the end of the month.

John，我們有辦法在月底前拿到足夠產能，真讓我大大鬆了一口氣。

㊳patience：耐心

It takes a lot of patience to negotiate with the planners as most of them are very conservative.

由於生管多半較保守，和他們商量事情得多些耐心才行。

㊴effort：努力

Phoebe, we appreciate your efforts in helping us solve the problem so quickly.

Phoebe，非常感謝你努力幫我們迅速解決問題。

課文重點② Summary 2

While production scheduling tends to deal with short term or even daily problems, capacity planning solves problems on a long term basis. Capacity planning is done mainly in accordance with mid to long range demand forecasts. As it usually involves capital investment, sophisticated financial evaluations are constantly being performed throughout the process. The main challenge of production scheduling is to cope with sudden delivery demands raised by the customers. The planners will have to optimize the efficiency of the entire process by going into details such as breaking up bottlenecks, pushing out minor orders, regrouping facilities or workforce, or even adding shifts.

生產排程解決日常接單的交期壓力，在實務上產能規劃多屬中長期作為，從一季、半年、到一年甚至三年。主要因為產能規劃涉及資本投資財務考量以及對業務成長的預估，對於中大型企業來說都是重要投資決策，須經過層層審慎評估。因此對於短期甚至日常產能需求的變動，都是透過調整生管排程機制達成。無論是業務訂單的波動或是因應客戶特殊需求，都需要排程人員運用對現場生產動態掌握，以調整人員、設備、或提升製程效率的方法滿足客戶需求。

生管排程：愛莫能助 I wish I could

Eric：**Buyer, Baxton Computer (Singapore)** 採購

Alice：**Sales Rep, Ultimate Cleaning (Taiwan)** 業務代表

Phone conversation 電話交談

Eric：Alice, how soon can you ship the goods under our P.O. No.TS-120090-0630? I'm sorry to push you as I haven't received the O.A. from you.

Alice，我們 No.TS-120090-0630 那張訂單，你多久能出貨？很抱歉來催你，因為我還沒收到 O.A.。

Alice：No problem. For your reference, our standard lead time is four weeks after receiving your P.O. and we just confirmed a 21-day lead time by our O.A. BP605933.

沒關係。給你作參考，我們標準交期是收到訂單後四週。我們剛剛確認了 21 天交期，O.A. 號碼 BP605933 。

Eric：So it's three weeks. I'm afraid we can't wait that long. We need the goods in two weeks.

那是三週啊！恐怕沒法等那麼久，我們得在二週內收到貨。

Alice：I'm sorry to hear that. I'll check with our factory and get back to you as quickly as possible.

真是抱歉。我現在立刻和工廠確認一下，會儘快回覆你。

Eric：Thanks very much, I will stay on the line while you check.

多謝了，我不掛斷，會在線上等你。

Alice：We are very sorry. Our manufacturing capacity is too full to pull in your order.

真的很抱歉。我們產線實在太忙，以致沒法提前出貨了。

Eric：Oh, that's bad. My boss will be giving me a hard time for this as he did warn me about your capacity before.

那真的很不妙，這下我老闆肯定不會讓我好過的，因為他先前就警告過我你們產能緊。

Alice：I wish I could help you. It is mainly because of our limited manufacturing facilities.

我真希望能幫你，主要是生產設備受限的關係。

Eric：Then how do you manage this overloading problem?

那你們是如何應付這樣超載的問題？

Alice：It is tough. Currently we are running 24/7, non-stop, 3 shifts a day.

的確很棘手。目前我們全年無休三班制，24 小時不間斷作業。

Eric：I see. In such a case I guess we'll have to wait.

是這樣啊，我們也只能等了。

Alice：Again, we are very sorry but we've done our best and we appreciate your understanding very much.

再次跟你說抱歉，但我們確實已經盡全力了，也很感謝你們的體諒。

❶ short term：短期的

The boss wanted us to pay some more attention to the short term adjustment of our testing process.

老闆要我們多注意對於測試流程的短期調整。

❷ even：甚至

Mia, can you imagine, some of the rush orders we received even requested us to deliver in 3 days?

Mia，你能想像嗎？我們收到的急單當中有些甚至要求三天內交貨。

❸ daily：每日的、日常的

We hold our daily meeting at 8:00 in the morning.

我們每天 8:00 開早會。

❹ on a long term basis：以長期方式

Jacob, we're evaluating suppliers on a long term basis.

Jacob，我們以長期方式來評核供應商。

❺ in accordance with：根據、按照

Lily, please bear in mind that all of us were requested to do our jobs in accordance with the system rules.

Lily，請牢記，公司要求我們每個人根據制度規範做事情。

NOTE

❻ mid to long range：中到長程

mid 中間的、中期的。

Matt, our capacity expansion plan was based on many mid to long range sales forecasts.

Matt，我們的產能擴充計畫，是依據許多中長期業務預測來製作的。

❼ demand forecast：需求預測

Because of the booming economy, recent demand forecasts have been extremely strong.

由於經濟景氣活躍，近期需求預測都很強勁。

❽ involve：（動）涉及、牽涉、包含

Olivia, it would involve too much effort just to decide if we're to take these small rush orders.

Olivia，光是要決定是否接下這些小急單就太費神了。

❾ capital investment：資本投資

Hey Ryan, It will be exciting if you could bring in some orders that require capital investment.

Ryan，如果你能拿到一些必須做資本投資的訂單，那一定會很刺激的。

❿ sophisticated：複雜的、深奧的

Nathan, the mechanism of the entire production scheduling operation is quite sophisticated.

Nathan，整個生產排程作業機制是相當複雜的。

⑪ **evaluation**：評核、評價

Carter, in order to speed up decision-making, we'll have to finish the financial evaluation more quickly.

Carter，為了加速做決策，我們得快點完成財務評估。

⑫ **throughout**：到處、從頭到尾

Sofia, trust me. You'll receive urgent pull-in and push-out requests from sales guys throughout the year.

Sofia，相信我。你一年到頭都會收到業務提出緊急提前或延後出貨的要求。

⑬ **main challenge**：主要的挑戰

Ashley, the main challenge of taking charge of the operations department is to constantly maximize our manufacturing capacity.

Ashley，掌管作業部門最大挑戰是隨時保持最大產能。

⑭ **sudden**：（名、形）突然、突然的

All of a sudden, more than 10 rush orders, all from Noah Systems, showed up in the system.

突然間，系統出現超過 10 張來自 Noah System 的急單。

The sudden order cancellation by Logan Technology put us in an awkward scheduling position.

Logan Technology 突然取消訂單，使我們排程變得尷尬無比。

NOTE

⑮ raise：提出、提起

Emma, what are you going to do with the pull-in request raised by Ashton?

Emma，你準備如何處理 Ashton 提出的提前交貨的請求？

⑯ optimize：優化、最佳化

It is so difficult, if not impossible, to constantly optimize the manufacturing resources over a long period of time.

要長期隨時做到製造資源最佳化，即使並非不可能，也是極端困難的。

⑰ efficiency：效率

Amelia, working in my department, you need to be good in both efficiency and effectiveness.

Amelia，在我的部門裡工作，你得做出效率也要做出效果。

⑱ going into details：注意細節、逐一說明

Lillian, I wanted you to give me a general picture, but you're going into details instead.

Lillian, 我要你告訴我一個概況，而你卻一直在細節上打轉。

⑲ such as：例如、好比

Natalie, while trying to improve utilization, you'd better watch out for other things such as materials and workforce.

Natalie，在改善使用率同時，你最好也能注意到其他事情，好比說物料和線上人力。

⑳ break up bottleneck：打通瓶頸

Ella, you have to shorten the lead time by breaking up bottlenecks at the testing stage.

Ella，你得打通測試站瓶頸來縮短交期。

㉑ push out：延後交貨

Samuel, I understand your point, but to pull in your customer's delivery means pushing out certain others'.

Samuel，我理解你的意思。但是你的客人出貨提前了，表示某些其它客人的出貨就得延後。

註：許多產業慣用 "push out" 來表示延後出貨，其實這名詞源自 ERP 系統，也可以用 "push back"。在正規英文裡，push out 純粹表示「排擠」、「推出 … 之外」，並無「延後」意涵，只能延伸解釋爲將原本交期推出交貨排程 (schedule) 之外。

㉒ regroup：調配、重組

The boss asked us again to regroup the testing machines to clear the W-I-P quicker.

老闆又要求我們重新調配測試機，以便快點清掉在製品。

註：W-I-P 爲 work-in-process(在製品) 縮寫。

㉓ shift：工作班次

Mr. Ball, for your rush orders, we have been working 3 shifts since Tuesday.

Ball 先生，為了你的急單，我們從星期二就開始採三班制趕工了。

NOTE

㉔ too full to pull in：超載而無法提前

full 指產線滿載；pull in 指提前交貨，也可用 advance 或 accelerate。(too 形 to + 動) 語意說明：太 … 以致無法 …。

I'm very sorry Eunice. Currently our production lines are too full to pull in any orders.

真抱歉 Eunice，目前我們產線超載嚴重，再也沒法提前任何訂單了。

註：許多產業慣用 "pull in" 來表示提前出貨，其實這名詞源自 ERP 系統。然而在正規英文裡，pull in 僅表示「拘捕」、「進站」、「吸引」，並無「提前」意涵，只能延伸解釋為將原本交期拉入出貨排程 (schedule) 之內。

㉕ hard time：不好受（的日子或時間）

Sales department is giving us a hard time overcoming all the problems with their unexpected rush orders.

業務部門突然蹦出急單所帶來的問題，讓我們吃足苦頭。

㉖ I wish I could help you.：我真希望能幫你（這次沒法幫，希望下次能）。

㉗ limited：（形）受限的、有限的

Because of the limited space, we are forced to work in a jam-packed environment.

由於空間有限，我們被迫在十分擁擠的環境下工作。

註：jam-packed 擁擠的。

28 **facilities**：設備、設施

Joseph, we have the most advanced manufacturing facilities in our factory.

Joseph，我們工廠裡有最先進的生產設備。

29 **manage**：處理、管理

Taylor, it's your responsibility to manage the morale problem of your team members.

Taylor，管理團隊成員工作士氣是你的責任。

30 **overload**：過載、超載

Frank, I don't understand why you failed to solve the overloading problem of your purchasing team.

Frank，我實在不明白，為何你無法解決採購團隊工作過量的問題。

31 **tough**：棘手的、困難的

Megan, it's always tough to deal with day-to-day communications with salespeople.

Megan，應付日常和業務溝通是一件很棘手的事。

32 **run 24/7**：全年無休（每週工作7天每天24小時）

As a result of the ever-increasing sales volume, we've prepared to run 24/7 for the coming year.

由於生意量不斷增加，我們已經準備好明年全年無休運作。

NOTE

㉝ non-stop：不停的、不斷的

Hey Chris, please be considerate as the engineers have been working non-stop for you, OK?

喂Chris，請你多體諒好嗎？工程師已經日夜不停替你趕工了。

㉞ 3 shifts a day：一天三班制

We've been working 3 shifts a day since the beginning of the year.

年初以來，我們一直是一天三班制作業。

㉟ in such a case：在這情況下、如果是這樣

In such a case, all we can do is to wait and see.

在這情況下我們只能等著看了。也能用“in this case”。

課文重點③ Summary 3

Capacity planning may always run into a dilemma, i.e., keeping a maximum utilization rate on one hand and building up sufficient buffering capacity on the other. The business decisions required are definitely tough to make, as heavy capital expenditures as well as flexible labor force planning are involved. Capacity Planning aims to adjust the workforce and production process in order to reach a maximum use of company resources with minimum system downtime, minimum bottlenecks and maximum level of output. But on the other end of the balance, capacity planning also needs to accommodate contingent capacity demand in the case of an unexpected business boost. In the real business world, it is always a dilemma.

產能規劃往往會以兩難情境收場：企業一方面要儘可能提高產能使用率，另一方面還得建立彈性緩衝產能。從經營角度來看，產能規劃決策由於涉及可能的高額資本支出及人員招募，就必須藉由調整生產流程與生產人力，達成最有效的資源運用。同時，還得把系統故障停機風險與生產瓶頸降至最低，以追求最大輸出值。糟糕的是在天平另一端，產能規劃還得顧全來自於業績無預警衝高所造成的緊急需求。在現實生意情境中，這永遠是兩難。

產能規劃：備份產能 buffer – good and bad 1-3

Elizabeth：**VP Supply Chain, Exton Tech (U.S.A.), leading two team members, Hannah and Samantha**；供應鏈副總，與二同事 **Hannah** 和 **Samantha**

Joshua：**VP Sales, XTE Frequency (Taiwan)**；業務副總 **Joshua visiting Exton Joshua** 拜訪 **Exton**

Elizabeth：Good morning, Joshua. Welcome to Exton. Let me first introduce my colleagues Hannah and Samantha. They are responsible for the ICs and crystals & oscillators, respectively.

Joshua 早安，歡迎來到 Exton。我先介紹二位同事 Hannah 和 Samantha，她們分別負責 IC 和石英震盪器。

Joshua：Good morning Elizabeth, Hannah, and Samantha. Very nice to meet you here at Exton Tech.

Elizabeth、Hannah、和 Samantha 早安，很高興來到 Exton 和三位見面。

Elizabeth：The purpose of this meeting is to review the case that happened one month ago, when XTE failed to deliver the required quantity of crystals on time to our OEM firm QY in China. As a consequence, QY asked us to step in, despite the fact that XTE wasn't our direct vendor.

這次會議的目的是要檢討一個月前的案例。由於 XTE 沒能準時將我們 OEM 代工廠 QY 所需數量的石英元件出貨給 QY 中國廠，導致雖然 XTE 並非我們的直接供應商，QY 還是要求我們介入處理。

地主說明此次會議目的，爲檢討先前供應商失誤而造成生產供貨問題，並對事件背景大致描述。

Joshua：Yes, first of all, I'd like to apologize to you and all the Exton friends involved in the case for the troubles we caused last month. And on behalf of XTE, I'm very much thankful to Elizabeth for giving us an opportunity to explain what happened at that time and what we have done since then to prevent recurrence.

是的。首先對於因這案子而引起的困擾，我在這裡向你以及所有涉及此案的 Exton 朋友致歉。同時我也代表 XTE，感謝 Elizabeth 給我們這機會說明當時的情形，以及為了避免再發生類似情形所採取的措施。

廠商 Joshua 立即在第一時間公開致歉，並感謝對方給予這次說明的機會。由於會議性質屬檢討供應商失誤案例，廠商代表 Joshua 理應先行當面致歉，暖化會議氣氛。

Elizabeth：Thank you very much. I accept your apology for Exton. And we'd like to hear a little more from you about the case. But before you start, I'd like to emphasize that the incident did affect QY's production of our smartphones. Luckily QY found ways to fulfill our order on time. Otherwise, I'm afraid we would have filed a claim against QY. In such a case, the chain effect would have been huge.

謝謝，我也代表 Exton 接受你的道歉。我們希望能從你這裡多了解這案子，不過在你開始前，我還是要強調這事件確實影響QY 生產我們的智慧手機。幸好他們還是設法準時出貨給我們，不然的話，恐怕我們會向 QY 索賠，那樣連鎖反應就很嚴重了。

客戶也正式接受道歉。但也再次強調事件發生已造成嚴重後果，凸顯這次會議的任務性質。

Joshua: Yes, I fully understand the situation. Let me begin by explaining the root cause of the incident. With regard to the individual sales person's wrongdoing that led to your serious concern and action, I'll address it in the later part of the meeting.

是的，我完全了解這情形。我從事件的起因說起，至於引起各位嚴重關切和反應的個別業務人員過失，我會在會議後半段說明。

廠商將事件起因分割爲人爲疏失及系統缺陷二方面，並打算將較嚴重的人爲疏失淡化，於會議後半段說明。這是一種先行設計好的策略。

Elizabeth：We don't mind, actually we prefer that you elaborate it first as we still find it hard to understand how a salesperson could act in such a way like that.

我們不介意，事實上我們還比較希望你先說明這一部份，因為還是很難理解一位業務人員怎麼能那樣處理事情。

不過客戶顯然也有定見並持相反意見，雙方都很有經驗。

Joshua：OK, I'll do it now. The reason that she behaved so weird was a lack of management. Being her direct manager, I should have prevented it from happening. But for some reason I didn't, though I did all I possibly could afterward to resolve the problem.

好的，我現在就說明。能用來解釋那位業務小姐怪異舉動的理由就是缺乏管理。身為她直接主管，我本來應該要預防這種事發生。但由於某些原因我沒能做到，雖然事後我盡了全力解決問題。

Dr. Lee 解析

廠商 Joshua 同意並擔下全部責任，而沒在業務個人失職上多著墨。這是因爲事件已過，個別業務人員過失在事發當時及事後都已經詳細說明過，不必主動再提。

Elizabeth: Please don't get me wrong as we don't intend to blame you now. Actually I did appreciate that you took over from that saleslady and responded with perfect timing. What we are more concerned with is how you're going to manage in the future.

請別誤會，我們並無意現在來責怪你。事實上我很感謝你當時能接手處理，而在最好的時機做出回應。我們現在比較關心未來你們要如何來防止。

客戶表示無意再責難，但希望了解未來如何避免再犯。

Joshua: Right. From the slide you'll see that I tackled the case with these remedial measures. First, I made a personnel change by sending Nicole Cheng to take care of QY right away. Meanwhile, taking this opportunity, we worked out an SOP for any similar case in the future. Most importantly, I started to build up a knowledge management system within the sales department.

好。從這張投影片能看到我採取這些補救措施：首先我做了人事更動，立刻改由 Nicole Cheng 來服務 QY。同時，借此機會我們訂出了一套標準作業流程，做為未來類似案件參考。最重要的是，我開始在業務部門裡建立知識管理制度。

廠商 Joshua 說明處理方式，包括治標（更換負責業務人員）與治本（強化管理系統與人員訓練）。

Elizabeth：Sounds nice to me. Please give us a brief introduction of this KM system. I think it's very creative and useful.

聽起來很棒啊。請簡短介紹這知識管理給我們聽吧，我認為那很有創意而且實用。

Joshua：No problem. Basically what went into my mind was a database with which the users, including salespeople, customer service staffs, and application engineers, interact to gain knowledge about their work on a day-to-day basis. Contents include operating process, case studies, professional expertise, and so on.

沒問題。基本上我想的是一個資料庫的概念，使用者包括業務人員、客服人員、和應用工程師，藉由互動獲得自己日常工作上用到的知識。內容則包括作業流程、個案研討、專業技術等等。

Elizabeth：Wow, that's impressive. We at Exton have also adopted KM for quite some time. It really helped us grow in every aspect of our work. So, Joshua, you're expecting your sales teams to benefit from it, aren't you?

哇，很棒！我們採用知識管理也有段時間了，確實能幫助我們在工作上全面求進步。你也期待 KM 能對業務團隊有所助益，不是嗎？

客戶也對 KM 表贊同，至此可明顯感覺會議氣氛更趨完滿。

：Yes, I do hope so, but I expect that the learning curve will be steep too. We've just only begun. I hope this answered your question about the personnel aspect of the case.

是的，我希望如此。不過我預期學習曲線一定會很陡峭，我們才只是剛開始而已。我希望這樣解釋能回答你對這事件中人為因素的疑問。

：Yes you did. I'm impressed. Now please go ahead with the system aspect.

是的，你的回答得很好。請繼續你另外有關制度層面的說明。

Joshua ：Speaking of the system side of the case, I admit that manufacturing capacity has long been our Achilles heel. We are constantly operating at a fairly high utilization rate which is not a bad thing. Yet we somewhat lack a flexible buffer to accommodate emergencies.

說起這案子的制度面，我承認產能長期以來一直是我們最大的弱點。我們隨時都處在高產能使用率狀態下，雖然很不錯，但是我們缺少彈性緩衝產能來應付緊急狀況。

接著廠商開始針對系統缺失進行說明，承認生產機制有難以克服的困難。

Elizabeth: It is crucial to us, I must say. QY has been doing an outstanding job in terms of both capacity committed to our regular forecasts and the flexibility to our urgent demand.

我得說彈性緩衝產能對我們很重要。QY 在承諾產能給我們常態預估和應付緊急需求兩方面都做得很好。

Dr. Lee 解析

客戶也表示，唯有消除這兩難情況方能繼續合作，客戶能明確指引正確方向也是一項收穫。

Joshua: I fully understand your position. As of now, to be frank with you, I still can't make a 100% firm commitment to QY for their capacity demand. In a rather unfavorable economic environment, it's always tough to make any decision on capital expenditures. Nevertheless, I'm determined to push for a much better performance in the future.

我完全理解你們立場。坦白說到現在我還無法在產能需求上 100% 承諾 QY。在經濟景氣不佳情況下，要做資本支出的決定一定很困難的。無論如何，我有決心繼續施壓，希望將來能大幅改善。

Dr. Lee 解析

廠商 Joshua 現實考量不願過度承諾，但允諾盡力改善。工業產品業績並非單獨能由個人決定而須依賴團隊合作，說實話是比較安全的作法。

: I understand the dilemma XTE is in. But if you're supplying components such as ICs and crystals, both capacity and buffering are absolutely essential if you want to continue as a supplier to our contract manufacturer, QY.

我能理解你們兩難的困境。不過身為零組件像是 IC 和石英元件供應廠商，如果想繼續和我們代工廠 QY 配合，產能和緩衝產能是絕對必要的。

結束前，客戶重申立場與未來雙方合作前提。

: I wish our CEO were here, although I know he didn't have too many options. Anyway, as the sales head, I need to get it done soon.

我真希望我 CEO 能在這裡，雖然我也知道他其實沒有太多選擇。不管怎麼說，身為業務負責人，我得儘早完成這任務。

NOTE

❶ run into：碰上、陷入

From time to time salespeople run into trouble by offending both the customers and the colleagues in supporting departments.

業務人員不時會陷入既得罪客戶又得罪自家同事的麻煩裡。

❷ dilemma：困境、兩難情境

To pursue a maximum market share and achieve maximum profitability is a dilemma to most companies.

對大多數公司來說，追求最大市占率和最高利潤率是個兩難情境。

❸ sufficient：充分的、足夠的

We offered ATT Tooling sufficient capacity for their Q3 forecast.

我們提供充分產能給 ATT Tooling Q3 的訂單預估。

❹ buffering capacity：緩衝產能

George, you need to figure out how we could build up enough buffering capacity.

George，你得想出我們建立緩衝產能的方法。

❺ definitely：一定、肯定

Sandy, we'll definitely be overloading next week.

Sandy，下星期我們必定超載。

❻ **capital expenditure**：資本支出

Christopher, I need you to give me a forecast on our capital expenditures for the coming year.

Christopher，我要你給我明年我們資本支出的預估。

❼ **as well as**：和、也

Ted, CRM as well as SCM is being implemented in our company.

Ted，我們公司現在實施 CRM 之外也在用 SCM。

❽ **labor force**：生產事業裡多指作業員人力、經濟學則泛指勞動力

Jerry, make sure the labor force in our three plants is in good order for the coming peak season.

Jerry，務必確定我們三個廠的人力能妥善應付即將到來的旺季。

註：peak season 高峰季、旺季。

❾ **aim to**：瞄準、對準、致力於

CRM aims to strengthen the relationships with customers by providing smoother sales operations.

客戶關係管理系統藉著提供更順暢的銷售作業，致力於強化客戶關係。

NOTE

⑩ **adjust**：調整

Ben, aren't you going to adjust our materials level for the coming slow season?

Ben，你還不調整我們物料水準來應付即到來的淡季嗎。

⑪ **reach**：到達

Roy, please see how we could reach the 98% utilization rate that the boss has asked us to do.

Roy，請想想看有什麼辦法能將使用率提升到老闆所交代的98%。

⑫ **maximum**：最大的、極大的

Bob, don't worry. We've given our sales team the maximum authorization to compete.

Bob 別擔心，我們已給業務人員最大權限去競爭了。

⑬ **minimum**：最小的、極小的

Janet, we're supposed to maintain the existing utilization rate with minimum increase in headcount.

Janet，我們得在增加最少人力情況下維持住現有使用率。

⑭ **downtime**：故障時間、當機時間

Tyler, we can't afford to have any downtime after Chinese New Year holidays.

Tyler，我們承受不起在春節年假後產線上的任何故障。

⑮ **bottleneck**：瓶頸

Alex, we have a serious bottleneck at the temperature testing stage.

Alex，我們在溫度測試階段有一個嚴重瓶頸。

⑯ **output**：產出、輸出

Ella, we were requested by the boss to uplift our output by 20% immediately.

Ella，老闆要求我們立即將產出提高 20%。

註：uplift 提高、舉高、抬高。

⑰ **contingent**：可能偶發的、不可預測的

The supply chain department is well prepared for any contingent demand for additional materials during the year-end rush.

供應鏈部門已經準備好，能應付在年終趕貨時期可能突發的物料需求。

⑱ **unexpected**：預料之外的、沒料到的

The unexpected big order from Pinnacle Steel kept us super busy for two weeks.

Pinnacle Steel 意外的大單讓我們忙翻了二星期。

⑲ **boost**：提高、增加

The recent boost in sales made everybody smile.

最近營業額的增加讓每個人都笑開懷。

NOTE

⑳colleague：同事

Nancy and I are long-time colleagues.

Nancy 和我是多年老同事了。

㉑crystals & oscillators：石英晶體&石英晶體震盪器

㉒respectively：分別地、各自地

Allen and Julie take care of the system division and component division, respectively.

Allen 和 Julie 分別負責系統部門和零組件部門。

㉓review：檢討、回顧

Daniel, the performance review meeting will be held on Monday afternoon.

Daniel，業績檢討會將在週一下午舉行。

㉔fail to：無法、沒能

Sarah, bad news, sales department failed to provide us with a more precise forecast.

Sarah，壞消息，業務部門無法提供一份更精確地預估給我們。

㉕required quantity：所需的數量

David, the required quantity of aluminum enclosures should be much more than expected.

David，我們所需要鋁合金外殼數量應該會比預期高出很多。

㉖ **OEM**：原廠製造代工廠"**Original Equipment Manufacturer**"的縮寫

Pegasus Tech has been one of our OEMs in Asia for many years.

Pegasus 長久以來一直是我們 OEM 代工廠之一。

㉗ **as a consequence**：因而、結果

We've been in a serious draught recently. As a consequence, we were forced to cut down the water usage in the process.

由於近來的嚴重乾旱，我們被迫在製程中減少用水。

㉘ **step in**：插手、介入

Mark, we'll definitely step in if the problem persists.

Mark，如果問題持續，我們絕對會介入。

㉙ **vendor**：供應商

也可說 supplier。

It is our policy to limit the number of vendors to 3 for each key component.

我們的政策是將主要零組件供應商限制在 3 家以內。

㉚ **first of all**：首先

First of all, I'd like to emphasize the importance of committing capacity to our tier one, AAA grade accounts.

首先，我想強調承諾產能給我們第一階 AAA 等級客戶的重要性。

NOTE

㉛ **involve**：涉及、連累、包括

Ruby, please make sure to send my message to all the colleagues involved in this incident.

Ruby，請務必要把我的訊息傳給每位涉及這起事件的同事。

㉜ **cause**：引起、使發生

Helen, I realize the shortfall must have caused you lots of trouble.

Helen，我明白數量短少必定已經造成你們很大麻煩了。

㉝ **on behalf of**：代表

On behalf of the entire Supply Chain team, I thank you very much for your timely support.

僅代表我們全體供應鍊團隊，我對你們及時的支援表示萬分謝意。

㉞ **thankful**：感謝的、感激的

Michael, we are so thankful to you for delivering the parts in time.

Michael，我們非常感激你能及時送來零件。

㉟ **prevent recurrence**：防止再發生

Brett, we'll do everything possible to prevent recurrence.

Brett，我們會盡一切可能防止事情再次發生。

36 incident：事件

Emily, the incident forced us to shut down production for 2 hours.

Emily，這事件迫使我們停機了 2 小時。

37 fulfill order：完成訂單流程、完成出貨的意思

Regardless of the shipping mistake, we managed to fulfill an order on time for Twix Foods.

儘管運輸上出了一點錯，我們還是設法準時出貨給 Twix Foods。

38 file a claim：提出索賠

We've just filed a claim for $100,000 with the shipping company for the cargo damage.

我們剛向船公司提出金額 10 萬美元的貨物損壞賠償。

39 in such a case：在這情況下、如此一來

I'm sorry, Ken, but we cannot accept a late delivery. In such a case, we will have to cancel the deal.

很抱歉 Ken，如此一來，我們得取消這筆交易了。

40 chain effect：連鎖效應

Robert, please pay close attention to the accuracy of your forecasts as it may cause a serious chain effect to us and to our suppliers as well.

Robert，請你特別注意預估的準確性，因為它可能帶給我們和供應商很嚴重的連鎖效應。

NOTE

㊶ **huge**：巨大的、龐大的

Gregg, winning Sun Steel's bidding will have a huge impact on our sales revenue.

Gregg，若能拿到 Sun Steel 的標案將對我們營收有極大影響。

㊷ **root cause**：根本原因

Richard, we must find out the root cause of the fire in our lab.

Richard，我們一定得找出這次實驗室失火的根本原因。

㊸ **with regard to**：關於、有關

With regard to the utilization rate, it looks really good now.

關於使用率，現在看起來真的很讚。

㊹ **wrongdoing**：過錯、不正當行為

Megan, we have zero tolerance for any wrongdoing such as bullying your co-workers.

Megan，我們不容忍任何如霸凌同事的不當行為。

㊺ **concern**：（名）關切、擔心

Morris, thanks for your concern for the system failure we encountered last Friday.

Morris，謝謝你來關切我們上星期五遇上的系統當機。

㊻ **address**：（動）提出、處理

Simon, let me address the capacity issue later on.

Simon，我稍後就會提出來談產能的問題。

47 mind：（動）介意、在意

Jimmy, before you proceed, do you mind telling me what your maximum capacity is?

Jimmy，在你開始之前，介不介意告訴我你們的最大產能？

48 prefer：較喜歡、寧願

Carlos, we prefer a longer warranty to a lower price.

Carlos，我們寧可得到一個較長的保固期而不是一個較低的價格。

註：這裡用 "prefer…to…" 而不是 "prefer than"。

49 elaborate：詳細解釋

Andy, regarding our QC systems, I'll elaborate right away.

Andy，關於我們品管制度，我這就詳細說明給你聽。

50 find it hard：指發現或感覺很困難的意思

I find it hard to finish the report in time.

我發現很難及時完成這份報告。

I find it ridiculous to know you increased the price without prior notice.

我認為你們沒先通知就逕行調高價格很離譜。

51 act in such a way：以…方式行事

Brian, about the incident, I have to remind you that you can't act in such a way in future.

Brian，關於這個事件，我得提醒你，未來不可再如此行事了。

NOTE

52 behave：表現

Julie, I like the way you behaved in the annual supply chain conference last week.

Julie，我很喜歡你上星期在年度供應鏈大會上的表現。

53 weird：怪異的

Cathy, the test data provided by Climax Chemicals looked weird.

Cathy，Climax Chemicals 提供的測試數據看起來很怪異。

54 a lack of：缺乏、缺少、不足

The biggest problem facing Debbie's team is a lack of smooth communications.

Debbie 團隊面臨最大的問題是缺乏順暢的溝通。

55 prevent … from：預防、阻止、妨礙

Steven, we need to prevent such a disaster from happening again.

Steven，我們得防止這樣的災難再次發生。

56 for some reason：不確定是何原因

For some reason, we failed to win the bidding.

不確定是什麼原因，我們就是沒能拿到那標案生意。

57 afterward：後來、以後

Anyway, Ryan apologized afterward for being rude to his colleague Maggie.

無論如何，事後 Ryan 為了他的魯莽向同事 Maggie 道歉了。

58 **resolve**：解決、下決心

Finally, our supply chain team resolved the materials shortage problem.

我們供應鏈團隊終於解決了原物料短缺的問題。

59 **don't get me wrong**：不要誤會、不要搞錯

Please don't get me wrong. I'm not asking for immediate delivery.

請別誤會，我並沒有要求立即出貨。

60 **intend to**：有意、想要、打算

Samuel, we don't intend to be critical, but you went too far this time.

Samuel，我們並不想存心挑剔，不過這次你們太過分了。

61 **blame**：責怪、怪罪

Grace, please don't blame Jessica as she didn't know anything about the material delay.

Grace，請不要責怪 Jessica，因為她完全不知道原料晚到了。

62 **take over**：接手、接管

Jack, since Larry is leaving the company, please take over his workload until we find a replacement.

Jack，由於 Larry 即將離職，請你暫時接手他的工作，直到我們找到接替人手。

NOTE

⑥③ tackle：處理、對付

Later, the boss asked me to explain how we tackled the issue.

稍後，老闆要我說明我們是如何處理這個問題。

⑥④ remedial measures：補救措施

Immediately after the accident, we worked out a complete set of remedial measures.

緊接著意外事件之後，我們制訂出一整套補救措施。

⑥⑤ right away：立即、馬上

After we complained to our vendor about the poor quality, they responded by sending the replacement units right away.

在我們向供應商抱怨品質不佳後，他們立刻做出回應寄來替換品。

⑥⑥ meanwhile：同時、在此同時

Our engineers just finished repairing the old machine. Meanwhile, we started to calibrate the newly installed machine.

我們工程師們剛把舊機器修好。在此同時，我們開始校正新安裝好的那台機器。

註：在多數時候，meanwhile 也能說成 in the meantime。

⑥⑦ taking this opportunity：藉此機會

Taking this opportunity, I'd like to remind you of the importance of an optimal utilization.

藉此機會，我要提醒你們維持最佳使用率的重要性。

NOTE

(68) **SOP**：標準作業程序，**Standard Operating Procedures**的縮寫。

(69) **most importantly**：最重要的

Most importantly, we must achieve the target of 100% punctuality of delivery.

最重要的是，我們得達成 100% 準時出貨目標。

(70) **build up**：建立起

Jonathan, the boss requested us to build up a stronger application engineering ability within the sales department.

Jonathan，老闆要求我們在業務部門裡建立起更強的應用工程能力。

(71) **knowledge management**：知識管理，縮寫為**KM**。

(72) **sounds nice**：聽起來不錯，口語中常用，是 **It sounds good** 的精簡說法。

其它類似說法有“looks great”看起來很讚、“tastes yummy”嚐起來可口。

(73) **brief**：簡短的

Sharon, would you please give us a brief introduction to our KM system?

Sharon，能請你簡短介紹知識管理系統給我們嗎？

NOTE

74 creative：有創意的

Frankly speaking, as a production planner, you don't have to be too creative.

坦白說，作為生管人員，你並不需要太有創意。

75 staff：職員、工作人員

All the staff in our department are female.

我們部門裡都是女性工作人員。

76 application engineer：應用工程師

77 interact：互動

Randy, the SCM helps us interact more closely with our suppliers.

Randy，供應鏈管理系統協助我們和供應廠商更密切互動。

78 gain：獲得、獲取

Zoe, we all gained experience from the mistakes we made.

Zoe，我們都從錯誤中獲取經驗。

79 operating process：作業流程

We keep our operating process as simple and effective as possible.

我們盡可能將作業流程保持簡單又有效。

80 case study：個案研討

Amy, a case study is a good way to learn and is also an important part of our KM system.

Amy，個案研討是一種學習好方法，也是我們知識管理系統中很重要的一部份。

81 professional expertise：專業技能

Ricky, most of us developed our expertise by taking professional training on one hand and by working smart on the other.

Ricky，我們多數都是一方面參加專業訓練，另一方面多動腦工作來培養專業技能。

82 and so on：等等、以及其它

Clint, our staff canteen offers light meals, coffees, snacks, and so on. Let's go eat there.

Clint，我們員工餐廳提供簡餐、咖啡、和零嘴等等。我們上那兒用餐去。

83 impressive：給人印象深刻、令人難忘的

Alex, your presentation was very impressive.

Alex，你的簡報讓我印象深刻。

84 adopt：採用、採納

We adopted a sophisticated forecasting module in our SCM system.

我們的 SCM 系統中採用了一個很複雜的預估模組。

NOTE

85 aspect：方面

As a junior planner, Denise is doing great in every aspect.

以一位新人來說，Denise 在各方面表現都很好。

86 benefit：（動）獲利、得益

Susan, the bottom-line is whether we benefit from the system.

Susan，重要的是，我們到底有沒有從系統得到利益。

87 learning curve：學習曲線

Our productivity is getting higher every week as we get further along the learning curve.

隨著我們學習更熟悉生產工序，我們的生產力每星期不斷提升。

88 steep：陡峭的

With our intensive on-the-job training for our production staff, we are expecting a steep experience curve.

透過密集內部員工訓練，我們期待看到很陡峭的經驗曲線（表示困難度高但進展快）。

89 go ahead with：繼續去做

Henry, we have to finish the meeting in half an hour. Please go ahead with the next case.

Henry，我們得在半小時內結束會議，請繼續看下一個案。

90 **speaking of**：說到、提起

Speaking of manufacturing capacity, Jason, you don't have to worry at all.

Jason，說到產能，你完全不用擔心。

91 **Achilles heel**：阿基里斯腱，指最脆弱的部位、致命的弱點

Lack of buffering is our Achilles heel.

缺乏緩衝產能是我們的致命傷。

92 **yet**：但是、可是、然而

Currently our capacity is full, yet we still have buffering capacity.

現今我們產能滿載，但是我們還有緩衝產能。

93 **somewhat**：有些、有點

As a result of several unexpected rush orders, we were somewhat panicked.

由於幾張預期之外的急單，我們顯得有些慌亂。

94 **accommodate**：提供、供給

In spite of our capacity shortage, we still managed to accommodate most of the demand.

雖然我們產能有些不足，我們還是設法提供給絕大部份的需求。

NOTE

95 emergency：緊急狀況

Don, in case of emergency, go and find Barbara for help.

Don，遇到緊急狀況，就去找 Barbara 求援。

96 crucial：重要的

Brenda, an optimal utilization rate is crucial to us.

Brenda，產能最佳使用率對我們來說太重要了。

97 outstanding：傑出的

Dan, your performance in production planning was outstanding.

Dan，你在生管工作上的表現太傑出了。

98 commit to：致力於

Dr. Lee has committed to R&D for more than 30 years.

Dr. Lee 致力於研發工作已經超過 30 年了。

99 as of now：至今、現今

As of now, we're still seriously overloaded.

至今，我們依然嚴重超載。

100 rather：相當

Yvonne, you'd better eat something now, as the meeting will be rather long.

Yvonne，你最好現在吃點東西，因為會議將持續很久。

101 unfavorable：不利的

Regardless of the unfavorable economic situation, we managed to hit the target anyway.

不管經濟情勢多麼不利，我們還是設法達標了。

102 capital expenditures：資本支出

Bobby, our capital expenditures will be at a record high this year.

Bobby，我們今年資本支出將創新高。

103 nevertheless：儘管如此、即使如此

Nevertheless, we are still aiming at a 98% utilization rate.

儘管如此，我們還是希望達到 98% 產能使用率的目標。

104 determine：下決心、決定

We are determined to overcome the difficulty in getting more buffers.

我們有決心克服擠不出緩衝產能的困難。

105 ICs：泛指晶片

Integrated Circuit 縮寫。

106 absolutely essential：絕對必要

Tommy, it is absolutely essential that we need to reserve more buffer for Kingtech if we are to meet our target.

Tommy，我們如果想達標，就一定得保留更多緩衝產能給 Kingtech。

NOTE

107 option：選項、選擇

Chris, I’m telling you. Giving up is absolutely not an option.

Chris，我現在告訴你，絕不可放棄。

108 get it done：完成（工作）

Max, it’s about time. Let’s get it done!

Max，時間差不多了，我們把它做完吧。

Lesson 2 Win by Capacity 產能與競爭

課文重點① Summary 1

For some manufacturing companies, capacity, just like pricing and VMI hub, has become an essential leverage in business bargaining. With a strong capacity support from the planning department, salespeople are in a much better position to build up competitive advantage for the company. Therefore, it is mandatory that salespeople are always informed of any updated capacity data, particularly if multiple manufacturing sites in different locations are involved. From the customer's point of view, it is absolutely a plus for the vendor to provide timely capacity information, to allow them to make a quick decision.

對許多生產廠家來說，產能就如同價格和 VMI 一般，已成為一項不可或缺的強力談判籌碼。業務人員若能得到充分產能支援，自然更容易替公司建立起競爭優勢。因此，讓業務人員隨時握最新產能資訊已屬絕對必要，尤其在多地多廠的經營模式下更應如此。而從客戶角度來看，若供應廠商業務能及時提供正確產能資訊，絕對是加分。

產能數據是隨身好幫手 make good use of it

Nicole：**Senior Buyer, Cambridge Electronics (New Zealand)** 資深採購

Walter：**Sales Manager, XTE Technology (Taiwan)** 業務經理

Video conference 視訊會議

Walter：Hi Nicole, can we start looking into details of the switch project we discussed last week?
嗨 Nicole，我們可以開始研究上週所討論的開關專案細節了嗎？

Nicole：Morning Walter. Sure we can. However, I need to know your maximum capacity first.
當然可以，Walter。不過我得先了解你們的最大產能。

Walter：For that specific model, the maximum combined capacity of our two factories is ten million pieces a year.
針對這個型號，我們兩個廠加起來的最大年產能是 1000 萬片。

Nicole：I'm afraid it won't work for us. That's not enough.
這樣的產能不夠大，恐怕沒法應付我們的需求量。

Walter：Then what is your requirement regarding this?
你們需求量是多少？

Nicole: We need a capacity of at least five million pieces a year. And that's one half of your total capacity.
最起碼的產能需求是每年 500 萬片。那已佔掉你們一半產能。

Walter: Oh, it won't be a problem for us because we can increase it by 100% easily.
喔，那不會是問題，要加大一倍產能都很簡單。

Nicole: Is that so? Please explain more about it.
是嗎？你能多解釋些嗎？

Walter: We are able to make quick adjustments to our existing manufacturing lines and increase our total capacity.
我們有辦法很快調整現有產線配置，來增加這型號的總產能。

Nicole: You mean additional capacity from your factories in Taiwan? Or from those in China?
你是指台灣工廠或是大陸工廠可增加產能？

Walter: As of now, it will be in our Shulin factory. However it won't be a problem for us to do it in our Soochow factory.
到現在為止只在樹林廠，不過如果有需要，蘇州廠也沒問題的。

Nicole: You have to be more specific on this. And we'd like to know some more details as it's so important to us. How about you come here next week and give us a presentation on this issue?
這點你得更具體說明才行。這對我們來說很重要，我們想多了解些細節。下星期你來做這議題的簡報好嗎？

Walter: Next week? It's tough. How about 10 days from now? I believe I'll have to discuss with our C-level executives before I start to work on my presentation.

下星期？很困難。不然 10 天後好了，我想這種大事我得和高層主管們討論過才能開始準備簡報。

Nicole：Fair enough. Call me once you have a date. And please bear in mind that we also need you to commit capacity direct from China. Please include it in your plan.

好，很合理。日子決定後告訴我，也請記住，你們也得直接從大陸廠保證產能，記得把這點放到簡報裡。

Walter：Sure I will. Thanks very much.

好，我會的，多謝。

NOTE

❶VMI hub：受供應商管理的庫存倉，為**Vendor Managed Inventory**縮寫。

Tim, General Instruments asked us to include a VMI hub in our proposal. We'd better be cautious about this.

Tim，General Instruments 要我們把 VMI 倉納入提案裡，我們最好謹慎些。

VMI 多為供應廠商受客戶要求，在客戶生產廠附近設立庫存倉庫，方便客戶有需要時及時就近提領使用。廠商則定期檢查庫存水準，做必要管理與補充。

❷essential：必要的、不可少的

Nowadays, keeping flexibility in production scheduling is absolutely essential.

現今，維持彈性生產排程是絕對必要的。

❸ **leverage**：力量、影響力、經由槓桿作用所增加的力

As expected, our operating scale served as the critical leverage in winning the business.

一如所料，我們的營運規模是贏得訂單的一項關鍵力量。

❹ **bargain**：議價、談判

Among so many business terms, manufacturing capacity is one of the most powerful weapons in bargaining.

進行議價時，在諸多生意條件中，產能是最有影響力的武器之一。

❺ **in a much better position**：處於更有利狀況下

Jack, once I receive detailed information about our capacity, we'll be in a much better position to discuss the subject when we visit Charlie Thompson next week.

Jack，一旦我們把詳細產能數據拿到手，下星期拜訪 Charlie Thompson 討論時，情況會對我們更有利。

❻ **competitive advantage**：競爭優勢

Julie, not competing with our customers has been one of our most valuable competitive advantages.

Julie，不和我們自家客戶競爭，一直以來都是我們最寶貴的競爭優勢之一。

NOTE

❼ **mandatory**：強制的

Vincent, a VMI hub is always mandatory if we want to do business with those big IT firms like WD and SG.

Vincent，想要和資訊產品大廠如 WD 和 SG 做生意，VMI 倉是絕對必要的。

❽ **inform**：通知、告知

Sandra, please keep every team member informed of the upcoming ERP training next week.

Sandra，請把即將在下星期舉辦的 ERP 訓練課程通知每位團隊成員。

❾ **updated**：最新的、更新過的

Dustin, make sure you get the updated capacity data from Solomon before we go and visit WD tomorrow morning.

Dustin，明天出發拜訪 WD 之前，務必要從 Solomon 那裡得到最新產能數據。

❿ **particularly**：特別地、格外地

Elizabeth, please keep an eye on the stock level, particularly Model 341 and Model 621.

Elizabeth，請注意庫存水準，尤其是型號 341 和型號 621。

⓫ **manufacturing site**：製造、生產基地

Jeff, all three of our manufacturing sites in China are equipped with state-of-the-art DCS.

Jeff，我們在大陸的三座生產基地，都配備有最尖端的分散式控制系統。

註：DCS 爲 Distributed Control System 的縮寫。

⓬ **point of view**：觀點、看法

Angela, from my point of view, I think that we need to become more automated in our manufacturing process.

Angela，我的看法是，我們的製程得更自動化才行。

⓭ **absolutely**：絕對地

Ella, you absolutely deserve this promotion.

Ella，你絕對應該得到這次升遷。

⓮ **plus**：（名）加分（的項目）

To some big companies like Foxconn, a VMI hub is no longer seen as a plus.

對有些大企業像富士康來說，VMI倉已不盡然是一項加分了。

⓯ **timely**：及時的、適時的

Cindy, your timely reminder saved us a whole lot of trouble.

Cindy，你及時的提醒替我們免掉好多麻煩。

NOTE

⑯ start：開始

練習 start 句型 1，start 後接動名詞：

We already started implementing SCM last week.

我們已經從上週開始實施 SCM。

練習 start 句型 2，start 後接 to + 原形動詞：

Scott will start to test the newly installed automatic wiring machine this afternoon.

今天下午 Scott 將開始測試新安裝好自動焊線機。

⑰ look into：研究、仔細審視

Terry, about your proposal, we'll look into it as quickly as possible.

Terry，關於你的提案，我們會儘快去研究。

⑱ switch：交換器

⑲ specific：特定的、明確的

Olivia, please be more specific. You're confusing us.

Olivia，請更明確些，你把我們都搞混了。

⑳ combined：結合的、組合的

There are a combined number of 2000 employees in our two manufacturing sites in Thailand.

我們在泰國二處生產基地共有 2000 名員工。

㉑ won't work for us：在我們這兒行不通、我們不接受

Lily, what you just did over the phone to our supplier won't work for us here in Taiwan.

Lily，你剛剛在電話上那樣子對待供應商的行為，在我們台灣是不被接受的。

㉒ at least：至少、最少、起碼

No worries, Katie. We'll send at least 50 units to you right away for your urgent need.

Katie 別擔心，我們馬上會寄給你至少 50 顆救急。

㉓ increase…by n%：增加 n%。

增加多少百分比介系詞用 by。

Samuel, it's sad to hear that our inventory increased by 12% from that of last month.

Samuel，聽到我們庫存比上個月增加了 12%，覺得真難受。

㉔ make quick adjustments：快速調整

Immediately after the setback in failing to get design-in from Dell for our storage device XTA336, our marketing team made quick adjustments to the product roadmap.

在沒能用 XTA336 儲存裝置贏得 Dell 的設計承認後，我們行銷團隊快速調整了產品藍圖。

NOTE

㉕additional：另外的、額外的、附加的

Don't worry too much, Boss. We'll get additional capacity for XT by leasing from TYE.

老闆，別太擔心。我們會用租賃方式從 TYE 那裡拿到額外產能給 XT。

㉖as of now：此時此刻、由現在起

As of now, we're aiming at achieving a utilization rate of 95%.

此時此刻，我們目標是達成 95% 產能使用率。

㉗how about：如何？怎樣？

Ryan, how about we meet up in 20 minutes at conference room 302?

Ryan，我們 20 分鐘後在 302 會議室碰頭如何？

㉘issue：問題

Lucas, about the overheat issue, we need to work out a better solution ASAP.

Lucas，關於過熱的問題，我們得儘速提出較佳的解決方案。

㉙C-level executives：最高級經營管理人員

爲 Chief-level executives 的縮寫，指公司的 CEO 執行長、COO 營運長、CFO 財務長、CMO 行銷長、和 CSO 業務長等。

Sofia, many of Singleton's C-level executives are going to attend the meeting tomorrow. Please make sure that the data in our presentation is correct.

Sofia，明天會有許多 Singleton 的最高層管理人員到場，請務必確保我們簡報數據正確性。

30 **work on**：從事、在做…

Tom, you'd better start to work on the monthly report right away.

Tom，你最好馬上開始寫月報吧！

31 **fair enough**：合理、可接受

口語常用的一句話，表示同意並接受對方的說法。

Max: Bob, I can't make it by 3:00 but I'll do it by 4:00 instead.

Bob，我沒法在三點趕到，不過四點就可以。

Bob: OK, fair enough. Let's meet at 4:00.

好（合理），我接受，那就四點碰頭。

32 **once**：一旦

Samantha, please call me once you get the data from the system.

Samantha，一旦你從系統得到數據，就打電話給我。

33 **bear in mind**：記得、記住

Neil, please bear in mind that we'll have to respond to Becky in 20 minutes.

Neil，請記得我們得在 20 分鐘內回覆 Becky。

34 **commit**：承諾

Gregg, we have to commit whatever capacity Raytheon Tire has been asking for, in order to nail down 100% of their annual order.

Gregg，我們必須完全承諾 Raytheon Tire 所要求的產能，以便吃下它們百分之百的年度訂單。

NOTE

35 include… in：包括在內、包含在內

Emily, please make sure you include our rolling forecast in the quarterly report.

Emily，請務必記得將我們的滾動預測放入季報告內。

36 sure I will：我一定會、當然會去做，口語常用。

課文重點① Summary 2

Within manufacturing industries such as semiconductor, IT products, consumer electronics and the related components industry, manufacturing capacity serves as the most critical competitive edge for the market leaders. To manufacturers, manufacturing capacity and yield require heavy investment in manufacturing facilities and technology. In return, the capacity and yield enable them to gain negotiating power while doing business with their giant multinational customers. Taking the semiconductor industry as an example, large fabless companies like Qualcomm, Broadcom, NVIDIA, and MediaTek rely on pure-play foundries such as TSMC and GlobalFoundries to supply them with the chips they need. Apart from these fabless companies, giant IT system companies such as Apple and Samsung also desperately look for maximum capacity from the foundries. Under such circumstances, the fabricating capacity and the production yield of the foundries become an important bargaining chip or a fatal weakness. In the end, capacity and yield determines the market position of the semiconductor foundry companies.

在某些主流產業如半導體、資訊產品、消費性電子、以及各相關零組件產業裡，產能往往決定生產廠家是否能成為領導者最重要的因素。生產廠家為了產能與良率，都必須進行鉅額資本支出，擴充設備或研發新技術。這類高風險投資所換來的是，藉由充足的產能與良率，取得與超大型多國企業打交道的實力。舉全球半導體業為例，大型無晶圓廠半導體公司，如 Qualcomm、Broadcom、NVIDIA、和 MediaTek，都依賴晶圓專業代工廠，如台積電與格羅方德，代工其所需要的矽晶片，每家都得爭取所需最大產能。加上如蘋果、三星等資訊與消費電子公司也同時需要鉅量產能。如此一來，台積電與格羅方德甚至三星的產能，自然就成為生意談判籌碼或是致命傷。因此，我們可說產能與良率決定了全球晶圓代工的市場秩序。

產能夠，再來談！ capacity prevails

Karen: **Senior Buyer , Cambridge Electronics (New Zealand)** 資深採購

Winnie: **Chief PM, Cambridge Electronics (New Zealand)** 主任專案經理

Nathan: **VP Manufacturing, Cambridge Electronics (New Zealand)** 製造副總

Walter: **Sales Manager, XTE Technology (Taiwan)** 業務經理

Walter is visiting Walter 前來拜訪

Karen: Welcome to Cambridge, Walter. We've been expecting your presentation. Glad you were able to make it so quickly.

Walter，歡迎來到 Cambridge。我們一直在期待你的簡報，很高興你這麼快就能來。

Karen: Let me introduce two of our senior managers. Winnie is our senior product manager, I believe you met before. Nathan is our manufacturing VP, and he is the guy who pressed me real hard for this meeting.

讓我來介紹兩位資深經理。Winnie 是我們主任專案經理，相信你們曾碰過面。那位 Nathan 是我們製造副總，也是苦苦逼我召集這場會議的人。

Walter：Thanks Karen. So nice to meet you Winnie, and Nathan.

謝謝 Karen。很開心和 Winnie 和 Nathan 見面。

Karen：We will focus on the capacity issue that I mentioned to Walter about 10 days back. As a consequence of the changes in our manufacturing resources and the ever increasing business volume we've received since the beginning of the year, our demand pattern for crystal oscillators has also changed significantly.

我們針對大約 10 天前我向 Walter 說到的產能議題來討論。由於我們製造資源的改變，以及從今年初以來持續增加的生意量，我們對石英震盪器的需求型態也跟著大幅改變。

Karen：Walter mentioned to me last time that XTE was flexible enough to meet our upcoming demand direct from China. We all believe a detailed discussion is essential. So Walter, you may proceed now.

上回 Walter 曾說 XTE 產能調整很靈活，有辦法滿足我們未來的需求，甚至連我們在中國的直接需求也沒問題。我們認為有必要來詳細討論。好 Walter，請開始吧。

因此，特邀零組件廠商代表前來說明未來產能重新配置細節。

Walter：Thanks so much for the briefing. And if you guys have any questions, please interrupt me at any time.

謝謝你的說明。如果大家在我說明過程中有任何問題，可以隨時打斷。

Karen: We'll be very harsh with you. Don't worry. I'm just kidding.

我們絕對會很嚴厲。別擔心，我是在開玩笑的。

會議氣氛顯然很輕鬆，顯示 Walter 與客戶採購主管的關係良好。

Walter: Thanks Karen. OK, I'll begin by introducing our overall manufacturing capacity for these two crystals, OX and OY specifically. Altogether we're able to supply ten million from Taiwan and China under normal operations.

謝謝 Karen。我就先來介紹這二顆石英晶體 OX 和 OY 的整體產能。在正常作業情況下，我們臺灣加上大陸共可以供給一千萬顆。

Karen: As I told you last time, we need a capacity of more than five million. Winnie and Nathan, what do you think?

我先前告訴過你，我們需要的產能超過 500 萬。Winnie 和 Nathan，你們認為如何？

Nathan: Combining Taiwan and China, we need a minimum capacity of six to seven million. Specifically, we need 3.5 million for our two plants in China.

台灣加上大陸我們最少需要 600 萬到 700 萬的產能，特別是我們兩座大陸廠就要 350 萬產能。

Winnie: Well, Gemini will need an additional one million. We just finished kickoff with the customer yesterday.

啊，Gemini 專案還需要額外 100 萬。昨天我們剛和客戶開完啓動會議。

專案經理臨時提出額外產能需求。

Karen：Hey Winnie, I wasn't even in the loop? OK, meeting is over. Thanks for showing up. Don't worry, Walter. I'm just making fun of Winnie.

喂 Winnie，我都還在狀況外耶！好，散會，多謝出席！別擔心 Walter，我是逗 Winnie 玩的。

採購對先前未被告知開玩笑表示抗議。

Winnie：It's my fault but please don't blame me. I'll explain to you in private.

是我不對，不過請別怪我，私下再向你解釋。

PM 表示私下說明，不要占用會議時間。

Nathan：Walter, can you break down your total capacity into Taiwan and China?

Walter，你可以將總產能分開成台灣和大陸二塊嗎？

Dr. Lee 解析

製造主管隨即切入重點。

Walter：OK. We have six million in Taiwan and four million in China. This is our regular capacity.

好的。我們台灣產能是 600 萬，大陸是 400 萬。這是我們正常產能。

Karen：It's not going to work Walter. You heard what our requirements are from Nathan. Your ten million aggregate capacities are by no means safe for us as we'd have accounted for almost 70% of it.

Walter，那樣行不通的。你已經聽到 Nathan 告訴你我們的需求，1000 萬的總產能太危險，因為單單我們就佔掉七成了。

Dr. Lee 解析

採購提出綜合需求，要求廠商提出解決方案細節。

Walter：I think that's why I'm here. And I'm about to show why you should feel more comfortable with our contingency plan. We have different plans for Taiwan and China.

我來這裡就是要說明這點。我正準備向各位解釋為什麼各位在了解我們緊急應變計畫後，應該就會放心了。對台灣廠和大陸廠我們有不同的做法。

廠商立即提出保證，先營造安心自在氣氛，表示問題能夠解決。

Karen: Good. I believe Winnie and Nathan are more concerned about it as a result of the additional requirement Winnie just mentioned. It's your show now.

太好了。由於 Winnie 剛剛才又提出額外需求，我相信她和 Nathan 會更擔心的。好吧，接下來都讓你表演。

Walter: I'll start with our plan for Taiwan. On top of the 6 million we now have, we'll get another 6 million from Trevor Electronics, a local crystal manufacturer with whom we've been working for many years. Currently, we're leasing their capacity for approximately 2 million low-end oscillators. This is an ongoing operation and Trevor also agreed to further support us with whatever the capacity we might need in the future.

我先從台灣開始。我們會在現有的 600 萬之上，再從 Trevor Electronics 那邊得到 600 萬產能。Trevor 是一家本地石英晶體廠，和我們配合已經好幾年了。現階段我們用租賃方式每年取得約 200 萬低階震盪器產能，這狀況一直持續著，而且 Trevor 也同意在未來全力支援，滿足我們所有可能的需求。

Nathan: I'm curious why Trevor has so much unused capacity. Hope it's not because of their financial difficulty.

我對於 Trevor 有這麼大閒置產能覺得很好奇，希望不是因為有財務困難。

PM 提出質疑爲何同行有閒置產能。

Walter：No, that's not the case. We've been working with them for more than three years. OEM revenue accounted for some 30% to 40% of their total revenue.

並非如此。我們合作已經超過三年了，而且 OEM 營收佔了他們總營收三到四成。

廠商據實回覆。

Nathan：Your plan for Taiwan looks fine with us. Do you agree, Karen?

你們台灣的計畫看起來很不錯，Karen 你同意嗎？

顯然客戶製造主管相當滿意。

Karen：I'm still a little conservative about it, but at least it looks better than I thought. Let's move on to your China plan.

我還有些保留，不過至少比我先前想像要好很多。下來我們繼續看你的大陸計畫吧！

採購亦表贊同，要求進入重點中重點，大陸產能。

Walter：We have two manufacturing sites in China, one in Suzhou and one in Shenzhen. Since currently we are already producing OX and OY in Suzhou plant, we're planning to add two to three dedicated lines for OX and OY with a capacity of six million to seven million . Before I came to this meeting, our CEO confirmed that decision had been made. We'll add two dedicated lines in Suzhou and start manufacturing OX and OY in 60 days. Meanwhile we'll have buffer capacity by making an adjustment to the existing lines.

在大陸我們有兩座廠，一座在蘇州，一座在深圳。由於蘇州廠現今已在生產 OX 或 OY，我們計畫再增加二至三條 OX 與 OY 專屬產線，產能在 600 萬到 700 萬之間。就在我出門來此前，我們大老闆向我確認已經做最後決定了，我們決定在蘇州廠增加二條專屬產線，並在兩個月後開始量產。同時我們會以調整現有配置方式保持緩衝產能。

Dr. Lee 解析

廠商 Walter 立即說明大陸增加產能方法（增加產線），並提出時間表。

Nathan：So altogether you'll have 6 to 7 million from Suzhou plant. That's great Karen, isn't it? It seems to me our most urgent concern will be properly dealt with, at least for the coming year.

所以你們在蘇州廠將有600萬到700萬產能。Karen，真不錯，不是嗎？至少看起來我們當今最擔心的事情能得到解決。

客戶製造主管再確認以避免誤會。

Walter：We do have full confidence in meeting your capacity requirements for the coming year, as the figures showed. And let me emphasize again that we're determined to serve you with all the resources we have. Do you guys have any questions?

就如這些數據顯示，我們絕對有信心滿足你們來年的產能需求。我再強調一次，我們會竭盡所有資源提供你們最滿意的服務。不知各位是否還有問題？

Winnie：I'm relieved a little bit. Thanks very much, Walter. And I'm impressed by the efficiency with which you set up two new production lines.

我算是鬆了一口氣，謝謝你，Walter！而且我對於你們增加產線的效率特別感到驚訝。

PM 表示安心。

Nathan：I'm totally OK. Thanks so much.
我完全沒疑問，多謝了。

製造表示完全 OK。

Karen：Nice presentation, Walter. I'll be working with you in the next couple of weeks to follow up on this. Thank you very much.
Walter 解釋的真棒！下來兩個星期我會和你一起解決這議題。真謝謝你。

NOTE

❶ **semiconductor**：半導體

❷ **IT**：資訊科技，為**Information Technology**的縮寫。

IT products 泛指資訊產品。

❸ **consumer electronics**：消費性電子產品如數位相機、數位電視等

❹ **related**：相關的

Additional capacity can be obtained by adding manufacturing facilities and the related workforce to the production line.

以增加產線上設備和相對工作人員，就能得到額外產能。

5 component：零組件

The passives and the actives are the two main electronic components.

被動元件和主動元件是二種主要的電子零組件。

6 critical：重要的、關鍵的

Daniel, sometimes offering VMI hub to customers can be critical to winning the business.

Daniel，有時候，提供 VMI 倉成為贏得生意的關鍵點。

7 competitive edge：競爭優勢

One of the most important competitive edges is our ability to provide application support.

我們在應用支援上的能力是一項重要競爭優勢。

8 yield：良率

或 yield rate。

Sammi, yield is one of the most important KPIs for process engineers.

Sammi，良率是製程工程師最重要績效指標之一。

9 facility：設備、設施

Mr. Lin, most of the manufacturing equipment that you saw was imported from Germany.

Lin 先生，你看到的生產設備絕大多數都是由德國進口。

NOTE

⑩in return：作為回報、作為替換、反過來

I delegated a lot more power to Jessica. In return, she leads the cleanroom technician team very well.

我大方授權給 Jessica，回頭來她把無塵室技術人員帶得真好。

⑪enable：使…能夠

The additional capacity enables us to win the lion's share of GE's business.

額外增加的產能讓我能贏得 GE 絕大部份生意。

⑫negotiating power：協商實力、談判實力

Making sure we've obtained a huge capacity on top of our regular one, I'm glad now that we have a very solid negotiating power.

確定我們拿到額外大產能後，很高興我們現在的協商實力更雄厚了。

⑬giant：巨大的、龐大的

Ethan, bear in mind that we're facing competition direct from a giant conglomerate.

Ethan 記住，我們得面對一家巨型集團公司直接的競爭。

⑭multinational：（名）跨國公司

Linda, our materials manager, has more than 10 years' experience in a couple of multinationals.

我們物料經理 Linda 有在兩家跨國公司工作 10 年以上經驗。

⑮ **taking…as an example**：以…為例、拿…來說

Taking myself as an example, I'm an industrial sales guy and an FAE at the same time.

拿我自己來說，我是工業業務，同時也是應用工程師。

⑯ **fabless company**：無晶圓廠半導體公司

fab 指 fabrication plant，而 fabless 就是 without a fabrication plant。

⑰ **rely on**：依賴、依靠

Bosco, being a manufacturing company, we rely on materials suppliers, and vice versa.

Bosco，身為製造廠商，我們依賴原料供應商，反之亦然。

⑱ **pure-play foundry**：指純粹晶圓代工廠、專業晶圓代工廠

foundry：晶圓代工廠。

⑲ **chips**：晶片，指 IC 晶片。

⑳ **desperately**：不顧一切地、拚命地

All the customers have desperately been looking for capacity from manufacturers in the face of the fast business recovery.

由於生意景氣快速恢復，每家客戶拼命地向工廠要產能。

㉑ **under such circumstances**：在這種情況下

Mia, under such circumstances, we'll have to find a second source for this precision resistor.

Mia，在這情況下，我們得再找一家供應商買這顆精密電阻。

NOTE

㉒ fabricate：製造、裝配

Lucas, we need to find someone to fabricate the tooling quickly.

Lucas，我們得找人趕緊把模具搞定。

㉓ bargaining chip：議價籌碼、談判籌碼

Allison, don't worry too much, as we are having a killer bargaining chip, in the form of the number of EC approvals at hand.

Allison，別太擔心，我們手上握有 EC 認證數量這張殺手級談判籌碼。

㉔ fatal：致命的、嚴重的

Ashley, I must say John's mistake was fatal.

Ashley，我必須說 John 所犯的錯誤非常嚴重。

㉕ weakness：弱點

Kingston's only weakness is lack of buffer capacity.

缺乏緩衝產能是 Kingston 的唯一弱點。

㉖ in the end：終究、到後來

We were thinking of buying one more milling machine. But in the end, we bought two instead.

我們原本打算添購一台銑床，不過最後卻買了二台。

㉗ determine：決定

Whether we'll obtain a design-in determines the destiny of the project.

我們能否拿到 design-in 決定了這專案的命運。

㉘ **presentation**：簡報

Susan, one of my planners, is going to give a presentation on our contingency plan this afternoon.

Susan，今天下午，我們一位生管要做緊急應變計畫的簡報。

㉙ **make it**：完成、做到、趕上

Anna, we're glad your supporting team made it in time this morning.

Anna，真開心，你們支援團隊今天上午能及時趕到。

㉚ **senior**：資深的、年長的、職位高的

Eric is our senior product manager for mobile banking.

Eric 是我們行動銀行資深產品經理。

這裡 senior 有職位高低意涵而非年資長短。

㉛ **pressed…hard**：強勢逼迫、催促、壓迫

Bella pressed XTE real hard for the OCXO we ordered two months ago.

Bella 為了兩個月前下單的 OCXO 拼命地催 XTE 交貨。

㉜ **back**：「之前」的口語說法，也可用**ago**。

I remember that I talked to you only 3 days back.

我記得我三天前才和你談過。

NOTE

㉝ as a consequence of：由於、因為

As a consequence of the late arrival of stainless steel bars, we were forced to shut down our fabrication lines for 8 hours.

由於不鏽鋼棒材延遲運到，我們被迫關掉生產線 8 小時。

㉞ resource：資源

Sarah, in order to further lower the manufacturing cost, we must maximize the resource utilization.

Sarah，為了進一步降低製造成本，我們必須盡可能多運用資源。

㉟ ever increasing：持續增加的、不斷成長的

Terry, the ever increasing labor cost forced us to consider adopting more robots, specifically in the testing section.

Terry，人工成本不斷上漲，迫使我們考慮多用機械手臂，特別是在測試區。

㊱ business volume：生意量

Natalie, we have to be more flexible with Tennox Metal's delivery because of their huge business volume.

Natalie，由於 Tennox Metal 生意量很大，我們對他們交期得更有彈性些。

㊲ demand pattern：需求模式、型式

Ann, the demand pattern of each customer is different and unpredictable.

Ann，每家客戶的需求模式都不同也很難預測。

38 **crystal oscillators**：石英震盪器

39 **significantly**：顯著地、明顯地、意義深遠地

Recently our workload has become significantly heavier.

最近我們工作量明顯加重許多。

40 **mention**：提及、提起、談到

Amanda mentioned in the meeting that we lost MTK's set-top box orders to AXC.

Amanda 在會議裡提到，我們把 MTK 的機上盒訂單拱手讓給 AXC 了。

41 **flexible**：有彈性的、靈活的

Salespeople always complained that we're not flexible enough when scheduling.

業務人員永遠抱怨我們排程沒彈性不夠靈活。

42 **essential**：必需的、必要的

Sarah, it is essential that you respond to our customer's inquiries more quickly.

Sarah，你必需更快回應客戶的詢問。

43 **proceed**：開始去做、繼續進行

Kevin, you may proceed with the annual budget now.

Kevin，你現在可以開始做年度預算了。

NOTE

44 briefing：簡述、簡介

Samuel, a marketing lady from Salesforce.com is going to give us a briefing on sales automation this afternoon.

Samuel，Salesforce.com 的一位女行銷專員下午會來做業務自動化的介紹。

45 interrupt：打斷、中斷、打擾

David, sorry to interrupt you, but it's an urgent call from your wife.

David，抱歉打擾你，不過這是你太太的緊急來電。

46 harsh：嚴格的、嚴厲的、刺耳的

Tom, you've been too harsh to some of our suppliers.

Tom，你對我們有些供應商太嚴苛了。

47 kidding：開玩笑、捉弄

Ricky, are you kidding me?

Ricky，你是在開我玩笑嗎？

48 overall：整體的、綜合的、全部的

George, let's take a review of your team's overall performance first.

George，我們先來看看你們團隊的整體業績吧。

49 altogether：完全地、全部地

Dylan, how many product managers are there altogether in your department?

Dylan，你們部門裡總共有多少位產品經理？

50 under normal operations：在正常作業情況下

Taylor, we maintained a 95% utilization rate under normal operations.

Taylor，在正常作業情況下，我們能維持 95% 使用率。

51 combine：結合、聯合、組合

Combining our two sites in China, we're employing some 5500 people.

我們大陸兩個廠加起來共有 5500 名員工。

52 kickoff：這裡 **meeting** 被省略掉，啓動（會議）。

Dennis, when will we hold the kickoff meeting with Triton?

Dennis，我們和 Triton 的啓動會議在何時？

53 wasn't even：學習使用 **even**（甚至）在否定句內。

Even 緊接動詞之後：

Yesterday I didn't even have a chance to talk to Chris.

昨天我甚至找不到機會和 Chris 說上話。

Mandy, I didn't even have time for lunch.

Mandy，我甚至沒時間吃午餐。

54 show up：出現、出席、到場

After waiting for almost an hour, the courier truck finally showed up.

等了將近一小時，快遞公司卡車終於出現。

NOTE

55 make fun of：開玩笑，捉弄

Take it easy, Michael. I was just making fun of you.

別緊張 Michael，我只是開玩笑的。。

56 fault：過失、過錯

Victoria, please don’t try to find fault with our suppliers.

Victoria，請不要挑剔我們供應商到吹毛求疵的地步。

註：to find fault with 挑剔、吹毛求疵。

57 blame：責備、責怪

Dan, about the shipping delay, everybody knows that you were not to blame.

Dan，關於運送延遲，每個人都知道錯不在你。

註：此處 not to blame 等同 not to be blamed，但 not to blame 較常用。

58 break down：分解、細分成

Joshua, please break down your total sales forecast by models.

Joshua，請按照型號細分你的總銷售預估。

59 regular：正常的、常規的

Karen, OIML C3 grade is the regular version we offer to the customers.

Karen，我們正常提供給客戶的都是 OIML C3 等級產品。

60 it's not going to work：不成、行不通

Hannah stop, it's not going to work!

別再搞了 Hannah，那樣行不通的！

61 You heard what our requirements are

以這句話練習避免一個錯誤的說法：

You heard what are our requirements.（錯誤）。

正確例句：Susan, tell me what your Q4 forecasts are.

Susan，告訴我你 Q4 的預估是如何。

62 aggregate：合計的、總計的

Nick, the aggregate capacity demand of Q3 is much higher than we expected.

Nick，Q3 的產能總需求比我們預期的高出很多。

63 by no means：絕不、並不、完全不

Frank, your Q3 sales performance is by no means acceptable to me.

Frank，我完全無法接受你 Q3 的業績。

64 account for：佔（比例）

Overall, our OCXO sales revenue accounted for 40% of our total revenue.

整體來看，OCXO 營收佔了我們總營收的四成。

NOTE

65 about to：即將、正準備

緊接 “be” 動詞使用。

Thank God. We were about to give up hope when you called to confirm the on-time delivery.

老天爺保佑，我們正準備放棄希望的那一刻，你就打來電話確認能準時出貨了。

66 comfortable：自在的、舒適的、愉快的

Doris, make yourself comfortable. Barbara will be with you in a minute.

Doris，放自在些，不用拘束，Barbara 馬上就來。

67 contingency plan：緊急應變計畫

也可說 Plan B。

Brandon, you have to work out a contingency plan for stainless steel 17-4 PH supply by 12:00 tomorrow.

Brandon，你得在明天中午 12:00 以前，完成不鏽鋼材 17-4 PH 貨源的緊急應變計畫。

68 as a result of：由於、因為

As a result of my tight schedule, I can only manage to visit our overseas vendors in Q4.

由於太忙，我只能設法在 Q4 拜訪國外供應商。

⑥⑨ **on top of**：除此以外

Karen, on top of being too harsh to your colleagues, you also need to improve your efficiency.

Karen，除了對同事過於嚴苛，你還得改進工作效率。

⑦⓪ **with whom**：和誰

with whom句型學習：

AXC is a reputable crystal manufacturer with whom we have been doing business for more than 10 years.

AXC 是一家很有信譽的石英元件廠，我們和他們生意往來已超過十年。

⑦① **lease**：租賃

Debby, the lease on our No.2 plant will expire in six months. Please go find and lease a larger one ASAP.

Debby，我們二廠的租約再過半年就要到期。請你盡快去找一間較大的租下來。

⑦② **approximately**：大致地、大約地、近乎

Because of the monster order from Dell, we'll need to hire approximately 200 temps by the end of the month.

由於 Dell 的超級大單，我們在月底前得顧大約 200 名契約工。

註：temp 臨時、短期契約、派遣人力，為 temporary worker 簡稱。

NOTE

73 low-end：低階的、廉價的

Sales of our low-end sensors account for less than 10% of our total sales.

低階感應器的營收只占我們總營收不到 10%。

74 ongoing：進行中的、持續中的

Jason, how will the touch screen IC shortage affect the ongoing projects such as King 1 and Rock 202?

Jason，觸控 IC 短缺會如何影響進行中的專案像 King1 與 Rock 202？

75 agree to：同意、答應

Sandra has agreed to adjust her scheduling and pull Dell's XT0715 in by 3 days.

Sandra 已同意調整排程，把 Dell 訂單 XT0715 提前 3 天交貨。

76 whatever：無論什麼、任何

No worries Benny. We'll do whatever is necessary to get it done.

別擔心 Benny，我們會盡一切可能去完成。

77 curious：好奇的、好求知的

Mike, I'm curious how you made it in the end, with so little support from the engineering team.

Mike，我很好奇，你是如何能在幾乎沒有任何工程支援情況下完成的。

78 **unused**：閒置的、未使用的

Joan, we should probably try to ask TAS to sell us part of their unused capacity.

Joan，我們或許該要求 TAS 賣部份閒置產能給我們。

79 **financial difficulty**：財務困境

Hey Bryan, did you have any idea of Contex's recent financial difficulty?

嘿 Bryan，你知道 Contex 最近發生財務困難這件事嗎？

80 **that's not the case**：事實並非如此

That was not the case. 或 *That is not the case.*

81 **OEM revenue**：OEM 營收

OEM revenue has decreased significantly in recent years.

近年來 OEM 營收顯著減少。

82 **looks fine**：看起來不錯

Tim, your Q1 performance looks fine.

Tim，你第一季業績看起來不錯。

83 **conservative**：保守的

Pete, comparing with AXC, we here at ATE are much more conservative, particularly in terms of business development.

Pete，比起 AXC 我們 ATE 特別在新業務開發方面太保守了。

NOTE

84 better than：好過、優於

Good job, Grace. Your report this month is a lot better than that of last month.

Grace，不錯喔！你這個月的報告比上個月的好很多。

85 manufacturing site：製造基地、生產基地

Stan, we rationalized our production and designated our two manufacturing sites in China to produce most of our low end sensors.

Stan，我們合理調整了生產，把在大部分低階感應器分配在大陸二個廠生產。

86 dedicated：專屬的、專用的

Currently, we have three dedicated bonding machines for model VTH220.

現今我們有三台 VTH220 專用貼片機。

87 buffer：緩衝

Dennis, the FAE suggested that you install damping devices between mechanical frames as a buffer to absorb the side impact.

Dennis，FAE 建議你們在機械檯架之間裝上阻尼器當作緩衝，以吸收側向衝擊力。

88 adjustment：調整、調節

Grace, you'd better make the necessary adjustments and get used to the new environment more quickly.

Grace，你最好做必要的調整，快點習慣這新環境。

89 **it seems to me**：我認為、在我看來

It seems to me that we'll have a tough time going through the transition.

在我看來，在轉換期間內我們一定會很辛苦。

90 **urgent concern**：迫切關注

Chuck, our most urgent concern now is to ship as many sets of Dell's laptops as we can, in the face of the capacity constraint.

Chuck，現在我們最關注的是，在產能受限情況下儘可能多出 Dell 的筆電。

91 **deal with**：處理、處置

Johnny, take it easy. I'm guaranteeing that your requirement for additional capacity will be dealt with as a priority.

Johnny，別緊張。我保證優先處理你們追加產能的需求。

92 **full confidence**：十足信心

We have full confidence that our channel partners will serve the end customers well.

我們有十足信心通路夥伴們能讓終端客戶滿意。

93 **we're determined to**：我們有決心…

We're determined to achieve the objective of 40% profit margin by the end of the year.

我們有決心到年底能達成毛利率 40% 的目標。

NOTE

94 relieve：減輕、解除、使免除

The last-minute arrival of the long awaited sealants relieved Chris of a tremendous pressure.

最後一分鐘才送到的封膠，讓飽受煎熬的 Chris 瞬間解壓

95 impress：給…深刻印象

Kumatic Tech, our new CNC machine supplier, impressed our engineers with the quality of its technical support.

我們 CNC 加工機新供應商 Kumatic Tech 的高品質技術支援，讓工程師們印象非常深刻。

96 efficiency：效率

Hans, all three new CNC machines are high efficiency types.

Hans，這三台新購的 CNC 加工中心都是高效能機種。

97 next couple of weeks：未來兩週、未來數週（寬鬆解釋）

Linda just told me that she'll be extremely busy in the next couple of weeks.

Linda 剛告訴我她未來幾週將會非常忙碌。

Lesson 3 生產方式

To order or to stock

課文重點① Summary 1

Delivery lead time is one of the most important competitive weapons over which a manufacturer must have very good control. Most manufacturing companies prefer that customers buy as many of their standard products as possible, in order to be more efficient in production and more effective in shortening the lead time. Therefore "make-to-stock" prevails in meeting the fast delivery requirement of the customers, although it also creates a problem to manage the inventory. On the other hand, "make-to-order" saves the manufacturers from keeping a substantial stock, yet very often, it lengthens the lead time. For those customers that want customized items for differentiation purpose, a longer delivery lead time is usually unavoidable.

交貨期是生產廠家必須有效掌控的最重要競爭武器之一，多數生產廠家喜歡客戶盡可能多買標準產品，以提高生產效率並有效縮短交期。「存貨生產」方式雖然比較能滿足客戶對交期的要求，卻也經常帶來庫存管理的問題。另一方面，「接單生產」雖能降低庫存過多或不準所帶來的困擾，卻難免拉長給客戶的交期。

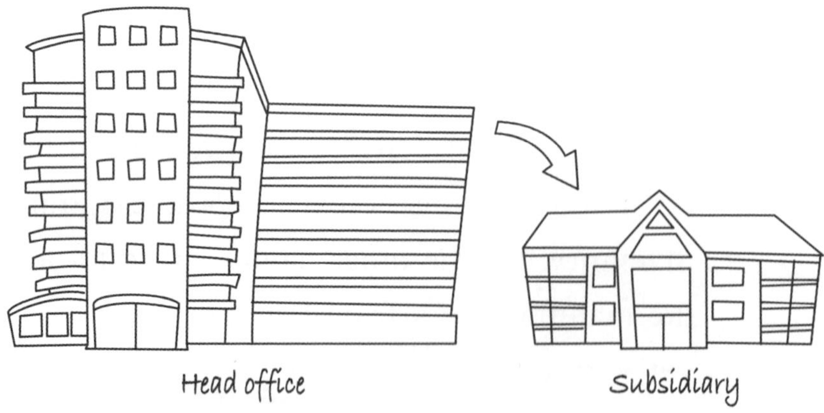

交期短與成本高的取捨 to keep stock or not

3-1

Amy : **Purchasing Manager, TransLink Electronics (Australia)** 採購經理

Daniel : **Sales Manager, Calcomm Technology (Taiwan)** 業務經理

Daniel is visiting Daniel 前來拜訪

Amy : Hi, Daniel, would you please briefly explain the way you will handle our orders in the future?

嗨 Daniel，能請你簡短說明未來處理我們訂單的方式嗎？

Daniel : Yes, I'll be glad to. If you order our standard products shown in our catalogs or on our web site, we'll do our best to ship from our stock.

好的，我很樂意解釋給你聽。如果你們訂購型錄裡或網站上的標準產品，我們會盡可能從現有庫存出貨。

Amy : What if we order more than what you have in stock?

如果我們訂購量超過你們庫存量，那會如何？

Daniel : Then we will start scheduling immediately, and hopefully ship the rest to you in 2 weeks.

若是那樣，我們會立即排線生產，希望能在二週內出貨完畢。

Amy : I see, a two-week lead time should be fine with us.

了解，二週的交期我們完全沒問題。

Daniel : But if you order anything other than our standard products,

you may have to wait for a longer time.
不過，倘若你們訂購的是非標準品，可能就得等久一些了。

Amy：I understand but how long will that be?
這可理解，但是會等多久？

Daniel：Well, it all depends. I would say between four and ten weeks.
這個嘛，說不準，得視狀況。我只能說，大致在四週到十週之間。

Amy：In other words, you have to do it from scratch.
換句話說，你們得從備料開始囉？

Daniel：Not really, we do keep sufficient key materials, but any changes in our standard manufacturing process will result in a longer production time.
那倒不至於，我們多備有足夠關鍵材料庫存。可是要在製程上做任何改變，都會拉長生產時程。

Amy：I see. And I guess it is the major difference between Make-To-Stock and Make-To-Order.
我明白。我想存貨生產與訂單生產最大差別就在這裡吧！

Daniel：Yes, you're perfectly right.
是的，你的理解完全正確。

❶ delivery lead time：交貨期

A six-week delivery lead time is too long to accept.

我們無法接受六週這麼長的交期。

❷ over which a manufacturer must have very good control.

學習介系詞在子句中的位置：介系詞 over 也能放在子句動詞 control 的後面變成 Delivery lead time is one of the most important competitive weapons which a manufacturer must have very good control over。

❸ prefer：更喜歡、比較喜歡、寧願

Jimmy, I prefer that you go and talk with your team members, rather than to complain to me.

Jimmy，我比較喜歡你去和團隊成員談談，而不是來找我訴苦。

I prefer to work overtime tonight, rather than to explain the delay to our customer tomorrow.

我寧願今晚加班而不願明天向客戶解釋延遲交貨。

I prefer holidays to overtime allowance.

放假或加班津貼，我比較喜歡放假。

❹ as many … as possible：盡可能多…

Bob, please try to get as many people to work the late shift as possible.

Bob，請盡可能試著多找一些人來上大夜班。

NOTE

❺ efficient：有效率的

Allen, you need to be more efficient in responding to the customers.

Allen，你回應客戶得更有效率才行。

❻ effective：成效好的、有效果的

Nathan, in order to be effective in lowering our inventory level, we have to ask our Tier 1 customers to place more blanket orders.

Nathan，為了有效降低庫存水準，我們得要求第一階客戶多下些長單。

❼ shorten：縮短、使變短

Cindy, George from Axton just called and asked you to shorten the lead time from 3 weeks to two.

Cindy，Axton 公司的 George 剛剛來電要你將三週交期縮短成二週。

❽ make-to-stock：備貨型生產、庫存型生產

Manufacturers plan their production according to the demand forecast. Once the batch production is completed, all the finished goods are sent to the warehouse as inventory.

廠商依據需求預估數據進行計劃性生產，一旦批次生產結束，製成品就入庫成為庫存。

The make-to-stock production may result in a high inventory cost if we fail to do a good job on demand forecasting.

如果我們沒做好需求預測，備貨型生產將會拉高存貨成本。

⑨ **prevail**：勝出、佔優勢、受歡迎

Speaking of corrosion resistance, stainless steel 316 prevails.

論起防腐蝕特性，316 不鏽鋼較優。

⑩ **to meet requirement**：滿足需求、符合需要

Do your sensors meet our requirement for corrosion resistance?

你們的感應器能滿足我們對防腐蝕的需求嗎？

⑪ **on the other hand** ：另一方面

On the other hand, we raised our ASP to protect our profitability.

另一方面，我們提高平均售價以保護獲利率。

註：ASP 爲 Average Selling Price 的縮寫。

⑫ **make-to-order**：接單型生產

Manufacturers start producing only after receiving orders from the customers. By doing so, there will be no inventory for the same item.

製造廠商只在接到訂單後才開始生產。如此一來，就不會產生任何該品項的庫存。

⑬ **save…from**：保存、解救

Jason's timely input saves our production from overloading.

Jason 的即時回饋訊息使得我們生產線不致過載。

NOTE

⓮ **substantial**：可觀的、大量的

Michael, I believe with such a big order, we'll get a substantial discount from our suppliers.

Michael，有了這麼大一張訂單，我們就能從供應商那裡拿到很可觀的折扣。

⓯ **yet**：但是、然而

We worked all night, yet we still need to test another 300 pieces.

James，我們已整夜趕工了，然而我們還有300隻得測試完畢。

⓰ **lengthen**：拉長、加長、延長

Our production engineers have successfully lengthened the life of our testing fixtures.

我們製造工程師成功延長了測試掛具壽命。

⓱ **customized**：客製化的

Grace, all the temperature chambers you saw here are customized.

Grace，你在這裡看到的全都是客製化溫控箱。

⓲ **differentiation**：差異、區別

There's little difference between these two torque wrenches.

這二把扭力扳手幾乎沒差異。

⓳ **unavoidable**：不可避免的

Joe, if the strike continues, shipping delay of our incoming materials is unavoidable.

Joe，如果罷工持續下去，我們進料延後將無法避免。

⑳ **briefly**：簡短地、短暫地

Gentlemen, we'll stop briefly at the next service area.

各位，我們會在下個服務區短暫停留。

㉑ **handle**：處理、對待

Dennis, I'll handle it.

Dennis，我來處理。

㉒ **catalog**：型錄

㉓ **ship from our stock**：由庫存出貨

We'll ship from our stock in a minute.

我們立刻會從庫存出貨。

㉔ **what if**：如果…怎麼辦？要是…怎麼辦？

What if we ship the goods from two different places? Is it acceptable to you?

如果我們從不同二處出貨呢？你們能接受嗎？

㉕ **in stock**：有現貨

Yes, we have plenty in stock.

是的，我們有很多現貨。

㉖ **schedule**：（動）排程、安排

Yes Martha, the meeting has been scheduled.

是的 Martha，會議已經排定了。

NOTE

㉗a two-week lead time：二星期的交期

形容「二星期的」要寫成 two-week。

a 10-day business trip

一趟 10 天的商務旅程。

㉘fine with us：對我們來說沒問題

Ella, you want us to hold the shipment? That's fine with us.

Ella，你要我們暫時別出貨？沒問題。

㉙other than：除了…之外、不同於

Other than those shown on our web site, we're producing many customized industrial PCs.

除了網站上那些以外，我們也生產許多客製化工業電腦。

㉚it all depends：視情況而定

Which one is better? It all depends.

哪個比較好？那得視情況。

㉛in other words：換句話說

In other words, we'll have to work overtime on Sunday.

換句話說，週日我們得加班趕工。

㉜do it from scratch：從原點開始做起、從零開始做起

Hey Tim, because of my inadvertent mistake last night, we'll have to do it from scratch today.

Tim，由於我昨晚無心的失誤，今天我們得重頭做過一次。

33 **not really**：不盡然

也可說 not exactly。

34 **key materials**：關鍵原材料

We have fairly good control over all of the key materials.

我們對所有關鍵原材料控制的相當好。

35 **perfectly right**：完全正確

Regarding work ethic, you're perfectly right about Sandy.

關於工作倫理，你對 Sandy 的看法完全正確。

課文重點② Summary 2

Inventory has always been a necessary evil for a B2B manufacturer, particularly in a slow-moving business environment in which customers are conservative in both forecasting and purchasing. Most of the time they place small orders frequently, but request quick delivery. And most dealers tend to shy away from keeping stock to avoid tying up too much of their working capital in the inventory. Under such circumstances, manufacturers have to maintain a balance between the inventory level and the delivery lead time.

對 B2B 生產廠家來說，存貨長久以來一直被視為必要之惡，特別是在產業景氣低迷時，由於客戶預估與下單都變保守，即使下單，也改成頻繁小單，卻往往要求快速交貨。另一方面，通路商更不願備庫存，以避免資金被綁死在庫存上。在此情況下，生產廠商就得設法在庫存水準和交期之間取得一平衡點。

砍庫存又保單 happy customers, little stock 3-2

Nick：**VP Sales, Campbell Tech (U.S.A. headquarters)**
業務副總

Monica：**Sales Manager, Campbell Tech (Taiwan branch)**
業務經理

Nick is visiting Nick 來訪

Nick：Hi Monica, the reason why I'm here is to tell you that we'll have a major change in our worldwide sales operations regarding local stock. I believe it will cause a certain degree of inconvenience to our customers, as well as to your team.

嗨 Monica，我來的目的是要告訴你有關我們全球在地庫存政策的一項重大改變，我相信那會帶給我們客戶以及你的業務團隊某種程度的不便。

總公司業務大頭來訪，說明新庫存政策。

Monica：It doesn't sound good to us, because local stock helps us compete quite effectively when considering that our ASP is about 20% to 30% higher than the alternatives. Please elaborate the change in detail.

聽起來不太妙，特別是我們平均售價要比同行高出 20% 到 30%，今天是因為有在地庫存，們還能有效在市場上競爭。還得請你詳細說明在地庫存會如何改變。

Dr. Lee 解析

分公司業務經理擔心原本售價已偏高難競爭，若庫存又受限，將會出問題。

Nick：OK, as you know, currently we're still keeping stocks in quite a few branches that don't have any manufacturing facilities such as Boston and Dallas in the States, Breda in Netherlands, and Taipei. We operated them as a regional hub of the American, European, and Asian markets respectively.

好。你知道目前我們還在幾處停產的分公司保留庫存，像是美國的 Boston 和 Dallas、荷蘭的 Breda、和台北。我們把這幾個點當作在美洲、歐洲、和亞洲市場的發貨中心。

Dr. Lee 解析

Nick 說明現今全球市場的庫存做法，在合併後，數個原生產基地依舊備有庫存，作爲地區性發貨中心。

Monica：Actually, all of them used to be manufacturing sites, serving a large number of markets and customers fairly well. For instance, we've been quite effective servicing customers in Malaysia, Australia, and Japan from Taipei so far.

事實上，這些據點先前都有在生產，並且提供服務給多處市場裡的許多客戶，舉例來說，我們台北就一直在服務馬來西亞、澳洲日本等地的客戶。

Monica 肯定現行作法的成效，還是不願輕易接受改變。

Nick：Well, yes and no, Monica. Our customers must be very happy that we served them well with our regional stock. But when we looked at the bottom line, we found it too costly to do that way. Actually we've been suffering a great loss as a result.
這個嘛，很不好說。客戶自然會對於我們用地區性庫存有效服務他們感到高興，但是當我們去看營運損益時，發現那樣代價太高了，我們實際上是在虧損。

Monica：Although I'm really doubtful about it, I'd like to know how we're going to change in the future.
雖然還是有些懷疑，我想了解未來我們會如何改變做法。

Nick：We're going to downsize or even terminate the inventory of all these branches to slash inventory cost. So in the future, there will only be three manufacturing sites keeping inventory for daily sales. They are LA in the U.S., Netanya in Israel, and Tianjin in China. Moreover, we'll have tighter control on the models and quantities that we keep as our regular inventory.
為了降低存貨成本，我們將減低甚至完全停止在這些分公司的庫存。所以未來我們只會在四處生產基地備庫存，因應日常所需。不但如此，我們還會嚴格控制這些庫存的型號與數量。

Monica：It isn't going to work, I believe. Definitely not for those popular items such as model 4410 and model 2263. How can we compete with a 2-week lead time against those who ship from their stock? To make matters worse, our price is 30% higher than their's.

我不認為那樣行得通，對有些常用的產品例如型號 4410 和型號 2263 絕對行不通。我們怎可能和那些能直接從庫存出貨的同業競爭？更糟糕的是，我們產品還比他們的貴上三成呢！

Monica 還試圖提出反對意見，表示如此一來，公司將更不具競爭力。

Nick：You're right about this. Therefore, you're allowed to keep a reasonable quantity of stock in your local warehouse for the commodity items like model 4410 and model 2263.

你說的沒錯，所以你們可以在本地倉庫針對大宗產品，如型號 4410 和型號 2263 準備適量庫存。

大頭說有配套措施，無需擔憂。

Monica：But how will "a reasonable quantity" be defined? Hardly are there any demand patterns to follow.

不過「適量」該如何定義？幾乎沒有任何需求模式可讓我們遵循。

Monica 持續質疑可行性。

：I'll assign a figure for you to follow. For the Taiwan office, the average inventory value in the past two years is approximately $600,000, according to the data provided by the finance department. In the future, you are allowed to have a maximum of $150,000 inventory value, therefore 25% of the existing amount.

我會給個數字讓你們有所遵循。根據財務部提供的數據，過去二年台灣的平均庫存金額大約是 $600,000，未來你們最多可備$ 150,000 的庫存，大約是現有庫存金額的 25%。

Nick 顯然有備而來，提出具體數據作爲執行依據。

：Oh no, Nick. In such a case, you'll definitely see a substantial decrease in our sales. We must realize that the only reason customers are still buying from us is that we have been able to satisfy their needs quickly enough. In other words, they pay a higher price for a better service. Now, if we stop offering our better product availability, why should they continue to buy from us?

噢，不成啊，Nick！這樣的話我們銷售額絕對會大幅減少。你得明白，現在客戶還願意向我們購買的唯一原因，就是我們還能快速滿足他們的需求。換句話說，客戶付較高價格換取較好的服務。如果現在我們不再提供較好的現貨服務，他們何必還要持續向我們買？

這是業務老招了，Monica 還是搬出掉單理由來反對，表示若無庫存優勢，往後將難競爭。

Nick: We can still do it if the customers could place blanket orders with us. This is a common practice in the States.

如果客戶願意下預估長單，我們還是可以備庫存的，在美國這是常有的事。

Nick 以美國長單作法要求 Monica 參考辦理。

Monica: Customers hardly do it here in Taiwan. It's not because they are not willing to do it. It is because their customers don't do it with them either. Most of them have little control over their own business.

在台灣，客戶幾乎不下預估長單，並不是他們不願意下，而是他們的客戶也不下預估訂單，他們多半無法控制自己的生意。

Monica 表示台灣情況不同，無法要求客戶提供長單。

Nick：Well, they have their problems, and we have ours to take care of. I've made the decision already, and we're going to carry it out. Otherwise, we'll be in deep trouble. And this is why we hired so many salespeople like your team and myself. We need to go and negotiate with our customers and get results.

嗯，他們有他們的問題，而我們也有我們的問題得解決。我已經下了決定要貫徹執行，否則我們會有大麻煩。這也就是公司要雇用你我來當業務的原因，我們得和客戶協商後完成任務。

Dr. Lee 解析

大頭哪是省油的燈，表示決策已定無需再多說，要求 Monica 馬上行動。

Monica：Certainly we will. I'll work with my team and try to find a smarter way to communicate with the customers. Hopefully we'll be able to receive more blanket orders from them. Alternatively, we may ask our dealers to keep more of our products as stock, for their own benefit.

那是當然，我們一定會去做。我會和業務團隊一起設法用較聰明的方式和客戶溝通看看。選項之一就是請我們的經銷商以利益考量多備些庫存。

Dr. Lee 解析

其實 Monica 也心知肚明，無法改變老闆決定，只能答應設法與客戶溝通，也可能從經銷商下手。

Nick：Yes, I think it is a better way than asking them for blanket orders. After all, keeping stock is one of the things a dealer is supposed to do.

沒錯，我認為要求他們備庫存的方法比要求他們下預估長單要好，畢竟備庫存本來就是經銷商的責任。

Monica：We may have to offer them certain incentives such as a special discount or a longer payment period.

我們可能得提供一些獎勵配套措施，比如優惠折扣或是延長付款期。

Dr. Lee 解析

老鳥 Monica 提出需要有配套措施做爲誘因。

Nick：OK, please go ahead and talk to them ASAP. We'll have to discuss this case by case.

好，那請你們趕快去談，我們可個案處理。

❶ **Inventory**：存貨、庫存

Bruce, we'll have to trim down our inventory level.

Bruce，我們得降低庫存水準。

❷ **necessary evil**：必要之惡、不可避免的災禍

Adam, I consider working overtime a necessary evil for a salesperson.

Adam，對一位業務人員來說，我把加班視為必要之惡。

❸ **slow-moving**：行動遲緩的、週轉很慢的

Annie, we need to get rid of that slow-moving inventory ASAP.

Annie，我們得儘速處理掉週轉遲滯的庫存。

❹ **conservative**：保守的

Daniel, to be frank with you, you've been too conservative in developing new business.

Daniel，坦白說，你在開發新生意上，一直都太保守了。

❺ **forecast**：預測

Alex, you have to be more aggressive in asking for a quarterly forecast from our Tier-1 customers.

Alex，你得更積極去要求我們一階客戶們提供季度預估。

❻ **place order**：下訂單，動詞用"**place**"。

Grace, please make sure to place an order with AXC immediately for 20,000 pieces of AT-24.

Grace，請務必立即下二萬顆 AT-24 訂單給 AXC。

NOTE

❼ tend to：傾向於

The planning department tends to maintain the original delivery schedule.

生管部門傾向於維持原有的交期。

❽ shy away from：避開、避免、規避

Because of the limited capacity, we tried to shy away from those low-margin orders.

由於產能有限，我們嚐試著不接那些低毛利的訂單。

❾ keep stock：備庫存、保有庫存

Benny, being one of our major distributors, it is your responsibility to keep sufficient stock for our business in Taiwan.

Benny，在台灣保持充分的庫存拓展生意，是你們身為主要代理商之一的責任。

❿ tie up：綑綁起來、綁死、套牢（資金）

We have been tying up too much working capital in the ever increasing inventory since last December.

自 12 月以來，我們已經有太多資金被綁死在持續上升的庫存上。

⓫ working capital：營運資金

The liquidity of working capital is extremely important to us in the face of an economic downturn.

經濟下滑情況裡，營運資金流動性對我們太重要了。

⑫ **under such circumstances**：在這種情況下

Under such circumstances, I have no choice but to terminate the agreement.

在這情況下，我不得不中止這協議。

⑬ **maintain a balance**：保持平衡

It is important to maintain a balance between production output and overtime.

在產出與加班之間取得平衡很重要。

⑭ **headquarters**：總部、總公司

通常用複數形。

I'm sorry, Jason. The hold instruction was from the headquarters.

抱歉，Jason。暫停出貨的指令是由總公司發過來的。

⑮ **branch**：分公司、分支機構

Yes, Lisa. We do have a branch office in Melbourne.

是的 Lisa，我們的確有分公司在墨爾本。

⑯ **worldwide**：遍及全球的、全世界的

The worldwide demand for CNC machines has been on the rise for several years.

全球各地對 CNC 工具機的需求多年來一直在增加。

⑰ **local stock**：在地庫存

No worries, Chris. We have what you want in our local stock.

Chris，放心，你要的東西我們這裡的庫存裡就有。

NOTE

⑱ cause inconvenience to：造成不便、引起不便

Mia, I apologize for causing so much inconvenience to you.

Mia，我對造成你們這麼多不便向你道歉。

⑲ as well as：也和…

Quality, as well as price, is what we are most concerned about.

就如同價格，品質也是我們最關心的。

說明：這句話是在強調 "as well as" 之前的名詞或主詞。

Profitability, as well as the sales revenues, is the key to our success.

就如同營收，獲利率也是我們能成功的關鍵。

⑳ it doesn't sound good：聽起來不妙

Dennis, it doesn't sound good from what I just learned in the review meeting.

Dennis，從我剛才在檢討會議中所了解的，那件事聽起來不妙。

㉑ consider：考慮到

Mark, I'd suggest that we commit the 10-day delivery to Aster for this rush order, considering their contribution to our company in the past many years.

Mark，考慮到 Aster 在過去多年對我們公司的貢獻，我建議答應 10 天交期給他們這張急單。

㉒ ASP：平均售價

Average Selling Price 的縮寫。

㉓ **elaborate**：詳細說明

Winnie, would you please elaborate about the plan you made for the coming trip to Malaysia?

Winnie，能請你詳細說明你即將出差馬來西亞的計畫嗎？

㉔ **in detail**：詳細地

Tim, I'm going to explain our contingency plan to you in detail.

Tim，我馬上會詳細解釋我們的應變計畫給你聽。

㉕ **quite a few**：相當多、不少

We offered such customized service to quite a few of our customers.

我們提供給很多客戶這樣客製化的服務。

㉖ **facility**：設備

Small as it may seem, we have here all the facilities needed for production.

這裡看起來雖小，我們有生產所需全部的設備。

㉗ **the States**：泛指美國，**the United States of America**

Doris is on a business trip to the States.

Doris 正在美國出差。

㉘ **operate**：運作

Our online service center operates 24 hours a day and 7 days a week.

我們線上服務中心每天 24 小時每週 7 天提供服務。

NOTE

㉙ hub：中心點、轉運站

Taipei is one of the major hubs for our global logistic service network.

台北是我們全球後勤服務網主要轉運站之一。

㉚ manufacturing site：製造據點、製造地點

After the merger, we have successfully reduced the number of our manufacturing sites from nine to three, worldwide.

合併之後，我們已經成功將全球製造據點從 9 處減少至 3 處。

㉛ for instance：例如、譬如、比方說

Ken, you should tell Dan exactly what we had to do for him to make that delivery. For instance, we resumed the night shift in order to accommodate his urgent request.

Ken，你應該告訴 Dan，為了趕交期，我們必須做些什麼。比方說，為了應付他的緊急要求，我們恢復了夜班作業。

㉜ yes and no：可說是也可說不是、說不準

問：Hey Andrew, is your business going OK?

嘿 Andrew，你的生意還好嗎？

答：Well, yes and no.

嗯，說不準欸！

㉝ bottom line：最重要的部分、企業營運的淨利、底線

Jack, to break even is my bottom line.

Jack，我的底線是損益兩平。

NOTE

㉞ costly：代價很高的、昂貴的

To deliberately seek out the low-cost vendors usually proved to be costly.

刻意去找低價供應商，到頭來往往反倒付出高代價。

㉟ suffer loss：遭受損失

Because of the prolonged economic downturn, we've been suffering losses for three years now.

由於經濟持續低迷，我們已經虧損三年了。

㊱ as a result of：由於、因為

As a result of the 7-day labor strike at the port of Oakland, we were forced to deliver some urgent shipments via air freight.

由於奧克蘭碼頭工人罷工 7 天，我們被迫以空運方式緊急出了幾批貨。

㊲ although：雖然、儘管

Although we ran into some testing difficulties, we managed to finish the batch on time.

雖然在測試碰上一些困難，我們還是設法及時完成這批生產。

㊳ doubtful：懷疑的、有疑慮的、不確定的

Eddie, I'm doubtful if the materials will arrive in time for production.

Eddie，我懷疑原料能及時運到趕上生產。

39 downsize：精減、縮小

To cope with the worsening economy, we decided to downsize the manufacturing.

為了應付日益惡化的經濟景氣，我們決定縮小生產規模。

40 terminate：終止

We terminated the agency agreement with Fulbright after they failed to achieve the sales target two years in a row.

在 Fulbright 連續二年沒能達成銷售目標後，我們終止與他們的代理合約。

41 slash：砍、削減

Emma, our expense budget was slashed by 30% vis-à-vis that of the last year.

Emma，比起去年，我們的費用預算被砍了 30%。

42 moreover：而且、再者

Julie, we're behind schedule, and moreover, we're having serious problems with temperature chambers 3 and 7.

Julie，我們進度落後，而且 3 號與 7 號溫控箱問題很大。

43 tighter control：較嚴格的控制

Team, from now on, I'm going to have a tighter control over your entertainment expense, as per the CEO's instructions.

各位，根據 CEO 指令，從今開始，我將更嚴格管制各位的應酬費用。

NOTE

㊹ it isn't going to work：不成、行不通、不被接受

I'm sorry Bill, as I said before, it's not going to work!

抱歉 Bill，我說過，那樣行不通的！

㊺ definitely：一定地、肯定地

Bruce, I will definitely give you an answer tomorrow morning.

Bruce，我明天早上肯定會給你一個答案。

㊻ to make matters worse：更糟糕的是

To make matters worse, we ran out of stainless steel 17-4PH bars.

更糟的是，我們缺 17-4PH 不鏽鋼棒材。

㊼ commodity items：大宗品項

Commodity items such as our model 4410 and model 2630 are being sold with extremely low margins.

大宗品項如型號 4410 和型號 2263 是以極低的毛利在販賣。

㊽ define：定義

Sam, it depends on how you define "hard working".

Sam，那得看你如何定義「認真、辛苦工作」。

㊾ hardly：幾乎不、很少

Hardly 起頭的句型說明：主動詞得放在主詞之前形成倒裝句型。

Hardly can I remember the type of the stainless steel we used for model 820.

我幾乎記不起來是用哪種不鏽鋼來生產型號 820。

50 assign：指派、指定

I'm going to assign Alex and Cindy to attend the conference next Tuesday.

我將指派 Alex 和 Cindy 參加下週二的會議。

51 approximately：大致地、大約地、近乎

Frank, we will need approximately 800 pallets for the shipment that is due to arrive on Friday afternoon.

Frank，為了星期五下午的進貨，我們大約需要 800 個貨板。

52 substantial：實質的、大量的

Through our team's effort, we achieved a substantial decrease in inventory.

經由團隊努力，我們大幅降低了庫存。

53 product availability：產品可出貨性

Susan, I just sent you a purchase order. Would you please check and advise product availability?

Susan，我剛剛傳了一份訂單給你，請你查明並告知何時能出貨好嗎？

54 blanket order：長訂單

Michael, under such circumstances, you need to place a blanket order with us.

Michael，在這情況下，你得下張長訂單給我們。

NOTE

55 common practice：常見的做法

I'm sorry, Ryan. It's not a common practice in the sensor industry to offer free samples.

抱歉 Ryan，在感應器行業裡，並沒有提供免費樣品的做法。

56 don't … either：也不

Emily said she didn't know what had happened. I don't know either.

Emily 說她不清楚發生了什麼事，我也不清楚。

I don't know either. 也能說成 Neither do I. 或 Me neither.

57 little：很小、極少

In the face of a power shortage like this, there's little we can do.

面對如此電力短缺，我們幾乎束手無策。

58 take care of：照料、處理、負責

I don't want to blame Ava, as she already had too much to take care of.

我不願怪罪 Ava，因為她已有太多事情要處理了。

59 carry it out：執行、完成

Guys, I fully understand your position. However, we need to carry it out anyway.

各位，我完全了解你們的處境，不過無論如何，我們得貫徹執行。

60 **in deep trouble**：有大麻煩

Ethan, if you keep complaining without generating any results, you'll be in deep trouble.

Ethan，如果你再抱怨個不停而又生不出什麼結果的話，你將會有大麻煩。

61 **get result**：做出成果、做出成績

Joseph, what I'm asking you to do is to get good results by the end of the year.

Joseph，我要求你做到的，是在年底前繳出成績來。

62 **certainly**：必定、一定

Hank, your failing to supply in time will certainly put us in a dangerous position.

Hank，你這樣沒法即時供貨，肯定會讓我們陷入危境。

63 **smarter**：更聰明的

We were required to work harder and smarter at the same time.

我們被要求更認真同時也更靈光幹活。

64 **alternatively**：可選擇地、二者擇一地

Alternatively Richard, you can send your FAE to repair the machine.

Richard，你可選擇派應用工程師來把機器修好。

65 **for their own benefit**：為了他們自身利益

They also raise their MSP for their own benefit.

為了自身利益，他們也提高了最低售價。

NOTE

⑥⑥ after all：畢竟、終究

Don't be too hard on yourself. After all, you've done your best.

別苛責自己，畢竟你已經盡全力了。

⑥⑦ is supposed to do：理應、被認為應該

Linda, make sure that you end the discussion by 10:30 in the morning, because that is what you are supposed to do.

Linda 你得確保在早上 10:30 之前結束討論，因為那是你應該要做到的。

⑥⑧ incentive：誘因、激勵

The sales incentive serves as an important motivator for the salespeople to perform better.

業務激勵獎金是刺激業務人員追求更好表現的一大動機。

⑥⑨ go ahead：去做

Vincent, please go ahead and take the order.

Vincent，去把訂單搶下來吧！

⑦⓪ case by case：依個案

Thomas, we'll discuss the special requests case by case.

Thomas，我們會依個案來討論特殊要求。

Page
Note

Lesson 4 Supply chain 供應鏈

課文重點① Summary 1

In a B2B business mode, relationships between the seller and the buyer can be a lot more complicated than one would normally imagine. Not only is the number of decision makers in the buying center larger, but the buying cycle is also much longer than that in a B2C mode. Moreover, the buying decisions per se are also a lot more sophisticated in terms of economic, technical, and personal considerations. For most industrial product manufacturers, it may take months, even years, to get a permit to knock on a customer's door. During the period, however, most marketing and sales people spend time and exert efforts building up relationships with the key personnel of the buying center. Relationship building is a long-term commitment made by both the seller and the buyer. It takes a ton of communications and interactions between the two parties.

在 B2B 商業模式中，買賣雙方關係的複雜程度往往超出想像。比起 B2C 模式，不但採購單位決策成員眾多，而且採購週期更是拉長許多。此外，從經濟性、技術性、和人際關係層面來看，B2B 採購決策本身的複雜度就特別高。對多數工業產品廠商來說，單單要取得與買方談生意的入場券可能就得花上一段長時間。這段期間裡，供應廠商當然都會使出渾身解數和採購單位的關鍵決策者建立關係。B2B 的買賣關係全靠雙方的長期努力，訂單肯定是經過無數回的溝通與互動後產生的結果。

VMI 非選項 a must or an option

4-1

Sandra : **VP Global Procurement, AOU Electronics (Australia)** 全球採購副總

Bill : **Sales Manager, Duke Technology (Taiwan)** 業務經理

Phone conversation 電話交談

Sandra : Hi Bill, I know what's on your mind now. And don't tell me I'm wrong.

嗨 Bill，我知道你在想什麼，你可別說我錯了。

Bill : Yeah, you're right, Sandra. Please reconsider adding us to your existing vendor list.

沒錯 Sandra，請再考慮把我們加進現有供應商名單。

Sandra : Yeah, I guessed right, but you know that it takes a lot of extra work just to prepare the documents, let alone ask our engineers and project managers to do the rest.

果然讓我猜到。不過單單是準備相關文件，就會增加好多工作，更別提還要請工程師和專案經理們搞定剩下的工作。

Bill : I fully understand that. And that's why we are prepared to offer you sufficient incentives to proceed.

我完全能理解，所以我們準備提供更充分的誘因，好讓你著手進行。

Sandra : Oh yeah? It sounds interesting. Please tell me about your offer.

是喔？聽起來蠻有趣的，告訴我是什麼誘因吧。

Bill：Firstly, our price will be 10% lower than that of your current suppliers.

首先，我們報價會比貴公司現行供應商報價低上 10%。

Sandra：I'm sorry, that's not too attractive. I'll let you know why after you finish this.

對不起，10% 不夠迷人哦！等你說完，我會告訴你為何不迷人。

Bill：And we will support you with VMI at the places designated by you.

另外，我們會在貴公司指定地點提供 VMI 庫存。

Sandra：Excuse me, what's VMI?

對不起，什麼是 VMI 庫存？

Bill：VMI means vendor-managed inventory. We'll set up the warehouse designated by you, usually close to your production site. You are allowed to move the materials you require freely from the inventory to the production site whenever needed. Meanwhile, we are responsible for maintaining the inventory at the agreed levels.

VMI 是指由供應商管理的庫存 vendor-managed inventory。我們會在貴公司指定地點設置專用庫存，通常距離你們生產廠很近，讓你們在需要進料的時候，可以就近由倉庫拉料上線生產。同時，我們負責管理，並維持一定的庫存水準。

Sandra：OK, we call it hub operation. Actually it's a must for each and every supplier. Is there any other incentive?

噢，我們是說 Hub 倉。事實上，這項服務是每家供應商都必須提供的。還有其他的誘因嗎？

Bill: These are the major incentives.
這些是主要的了。

Sandra: About your price, I'm telling you 10% reduction is too little to justify the extra work that our engineers will have to do.
關於價格，現在我告訴你，要我去說服相關部門同事加班去多做事，那 10% 不夠的。

Bill: May I know why?
能告訴我為什麼嗎？

Sandra: There will need to be a team of people involved with the whole process. The costs are way too high.
要知道，會有一個團隊成員投入這整個過程，投入成本是非常高的。

Bill: I see. I guess I'll have to come up with a more attractive package for you. I'll talk to you next week.
是這樣啊。我看我們得想出一套更誘人的方案才行，下星期再來找你談囉！

Sandra: I'll be glad to discuss with you about this if you are able to offer us a much more attractive price.
只要你能夠給我們更低、更有吸引力的價格，我很願意和你再討論。

NOTE

❶ B2B business mode：B2B商業模式

B2B 為 Business-to-Business 的縮寫。

❷ complicated：複雜的

Joe, things here are a bit complicated now.

Joe，現在事情變得有些複雜了。

❸ not only…but also：不但…也、不但…而且

Our ERP system not only runs effectively for production planning but also for material control.

我們公司 ERP 系統不但能有效排程，還能有效進行物料控管。

Not only did Sandy bring the spare parts with her but she also completed on-site replacement in 30 minutes.

Sandy 不但隨身帶著零件，還在現場花不到半小時就更換完成了。

Not only Susan but also Steven will attend the factory safety training program next week.

下星期不僅 Susan，Steven 也會參加工廠安全訓練活動。

❹ buying center：採購中心

多半不是指正式編制單位，而是指與採購決策有直接關聯的成員，如研發工程師、零件工程師、或專案經理，當然也包括採購。

David, please tell me who the most influential decision makers in Acer Steel's buying center are.

David，請你告訴我 Acer Steel 採購中心裡最具決策影響力的人是哪幾位。

5 buying cycle：採購週期

The buying cycle of a CNC machine can be as long as three to six months.

一台 CNC 加工機的採購週期能長達 3 至 6 個月。

6 moreover：此外、而且

Jim, the ultrasonic cleaner you bought last month worked so well. Moreover, it was so quiet while in operation.

Jim，你上個月購買的那台超音波清洗機很好用，而且運轉起來超安靜。

7 per se：本身、本質、自身

Alex, no problem with our capacity per se. It was the materials that caused the delay.

Alex，我們產能本身沒問題，延誤是物料所造成。

8 sophisticated：複雜的、老練的、世故的

The mechanism of this automated sorting machine is very sophisticated.

這台自動分級機的操作機制非常複雜。

9 in terms of：在…方面、就…而言

Buddy Steel has been one of our best suppliers in terms of delivery punctuality.

以交貨準時性來說，Buddy Steel 一直是我們最佳供應商之一。

NOTE

⑩ permit：許可、許可證

Nancy, we need to get a permit from the Customs Office in order to clear the goods earlier.

Nancy，若要早些完成清關，我們得拿到海關發出的許可。

⑪ knock on someone's door：敲門

Benny, I'm glad that after being listed on First Steel's AVL, we're able to knock on their buying center's door.

Benny，很高興在我們被放上 First Steel 的認可供應商名單後，可以去敲他們採購中心的大門了。

⑫ exert：發揮、竭盡全力

No worries, Rex. We'll exert our greatest efforts to pull in your order.

Rex 別擔心，我們會盡最大努力提前交貨。

⑬ key personnel：關鍵的人員

Randy is in charge of the PM department and is also one of the key personnel of our purchasing center.

Randy 是我們 PM 部門主管，也是採購中心的關鍵成員之一。

⑭ commitment：承諾

Ted is supposed to honor his commitment to push out our order till next month.

Ted 應該要兌現延後到下個月出貨的承諾。

⑮ **a ton of**：大量的、許多

Team, there is still a ton of work to be finished before we call it a day.

各位，在我們下班前還有成堆的事情得完成。

⑯ **interaction**：互動

The interaction between Cindy, our new planner, and the rest of the planning team is really good.

我們新進的生管 Cindy 和團隊其他成員之間的互動真的很好。

⑰ **procurement**：採購

Alyssa is taking charge of the procurement of all passives for our company.

Alyssa 負責我們公司所有被動元件的採購。

⑱ **what's on your mind**：在想些什麼、在打什麼主意

Samuel, don't try to fool me. I know what's on your mind.

Samuel，別想騙我，我知道你在想什麼。

⑲ **reconsider**：再考慮

OK Ethan, we'll reconsider granting you a special rate for this particular order.

好吧 Ethan，我們會特別針對這張訂單再考慮給你們一個特殊售價。

NOTE

⑳ extra：額外的、另外的

Sorry Dennis, I can’t leave now as I have some extra jobs to do.

對不起Dennis，我現在沒法離開，因為我有一些額外工作得做。

㉑ let alone：更別提、更不用說

Nick, it’s difficult to ship the goods to you tomorrow as we planned, let alone ship them to you today.

Nick，要按我們原先排定明天出貨都有困難了，就更別提要我們今天就出貨給你們。

㉒ incentive：誘因、激勵

Lydia, my team has been continuously under tremendous pressure for a long time. We definitely need more incentives if you ask us to work overtime.

Lydia，我的團隊已經持續背負極大壓力好久了，如果你要求我們加班工作，我們絕對需要有更多的誘因才行。

㉓ proceed：繼續進行、開始

Isabelle, you may want to proceed with your presentation.

Isabelle，你可以繼續做簡報了。

㉔ it sounds interesting：聽起來很有趣

Hank, it sounds interesting. Would you please elaborate?

Hank，那聽起來挺有趣的，能請你詳細說明嗎？

㉕ **attractive**：有吸引力的、迷人的

To be honest with you Jason, your quotation doesn't look attractive at all.

老實說，Jason，你們的報價完全不具吸引力。

㉖ **VMI**：供應商管理庫存或稱 **Hub** 庫存

Nowadays, offering VMI has become a must in order to compete in the consumer electronics industry.

當今消費性電子產業裡，提供 VMI 服務已經成為競爭的必備條件了。

㉗ **designate**：指定、選定

Xpress has been designated by us as the exclusive freight forwarder for our outbound cargo.

Xpress 已經被我們指定為出口貨的獨家貨運代理。

㉘ **set up**：建立、設立、開辦

We set up a liaison office in Rio de Janeiro last month.

我們上個月在里約熱內盧設立了辦事處。

㉙ **usually**：通常地、一般地

Linda, what do we usually do if a customer failed to pay on time?

Linda，如果客戶沒能準時付款，我們通常會怎麼做？

NOTE

㉚be allowed to：被允許

Because of the last-minute alteration of the purchase order, we were allowed to dispatch the shipment one week later.

由於客戶在最後關頭修改訂單，我們被允許延遲一星期出貨。

㉛whenever：無論何時、隨時、只要、每當

Monica, call or text me whenever you need me.

Monica，只要你需要我，就打電話或傳簡訊給我。

㉜maintain：維持、維護

Ashley, you need to maintain regular contact with our suppliers, large or small.

Ashley，無論規模大小，你得和我們供應商維持定期聯繫。

㉝agree：同意、贊成

Frank, I agree with you that we need to increase our MSP.

Frank，我同意你的看法，我們得調高最低售價。

Connie, I agree to your proposal of increasing our MSP.

Connie，我贊成你調高最低售價的提案。

㉞hub operation：hub 作業，等同 VMI 倉

Jimmy, in order to be qualified as a second source, you have to provide hub operation.

Jimmy，你們必須提供hub作業才有資格被列為第二供貨廠商。

35 **it's a must**：一定得、一定要、必須

Guys, it's a must that we finish all the testing tonight.

各位，我們今晚非得完成所有測試不可。

36 **justify**：證明有道理

Gary, I'll show you how the savings justify the extra efforts.

Gary，我會讓你了解省下來的錢是如何值得我們多付出些努力。

37 **process**：歷程、過程

Bob, we'll have to monitor the entire testing process very carefully.

Bob，我們得非常小心監控整個測試過程。

38 **way too high**：太高了、過高了

I'm sorry Dennis. The price you quoted is way too high to accept.

抱歉 Dennis，你的報價高過頭了，我們無法接受。

39 **I see**：我懂了、我明白了、原來如此

40 **come up with**：做出、提出、想出

Carl managed to come up with a proposal in two hours last night.

昨晚 Carl 想盡辦法在二小時之內趕出一份提案。

41 **package**：套裝提案

I'll take the job if the package is right.

如果待遇提案適合，我會接受這份工作。

課文重點② Summary 2

We've heard terms like 955 ATP or even 982 ATP in today's business environment. In such a scenario, the manufacturer is allowed only a few days for order fulfillment. As a result, most manufacturers want to seek co-operation from their major clients to create a more precise demand forecast, which therefore has become a lot more important today than in the past. Apart from the aforementioned demanding request for short lead time, it is also due to the complexity involved in modern supply chain management and manufacturing operations. An accurate demand forecast not only lowers the inventory level significantly along the supply chain, but also shortens the manufacturing lead time in a more effective way. It eventually leads to a more stable supply chain and this then benefits both the supplier and the customer.

在當今產業環境裡，我們不時會聽到 955 ATP（955 出貨承諾），甚至 982 ATP（982 出貨承諾）的名詞。在這種情境裡，製造廠商的交貨期只有短短幾天而已。因此多數製造廠商會設法取得主要客戶的配合，提供更精確的需求預估。比起從前，當今這類需求預估當然就顯得更為重要。之所以會如此，除了前述客戶要求交期越來越短的因素外，現今供應鏈管理和製造本身的複雜程度也是主要原因。一份精確的需求預估不但能顯著降低庫存水準，還能有效縮短交期。最終它更能使供應鏈更加穩定，而形成買賣兩方雙贏的局面。

快速出貨承諾靠 demand forecast

Greg：**Purchasing Manager, Pro-Maker Ind. (Australia)** 採購經理

Sandy：**Sales Manager, Luxent Tech (Taiwan)** 業務經理

Video conference 視訊會議

Greg：Hi Sandy, I just sent you our weekly forecast update. Please make sure to deliver all we need in the next couple of weeks on time.

嗨 Sandy，我剛剛把最新的每週訂單預估傳給你了，請務必要在未來二週內準時出貨。

視訊會議由討論每週更新預估數據開始。

Sandy：Hi Greg, yes, I received it. I can see there's a significant increase in your forecast. I'm wondering if such an increase will continue and how long it will last.

嗨 Greg，是的，我收到了，不過我看到預估數量增加不少。我正在想這樣的增加還會持續多久。

Dr. Lee 解析

供應廠商發現最新預估數據增加許多，想問清楚是否爲長期趨勢。

Greg：We just received a few rush orders. We have to deliver in three weeks from now. But it is still premature at the moment to tell if the increase is a steady trend. Don't worry. I'll keep an eye on this and keep you closely informed.

我們剛剛接到幾張急單，得在未來二週內出貨完畢，不過現在要斷定這是不是穩定趨勢還太早。別擔心，我會特別注意也會隨時讓你了解狀況的。

Dr. Lee 解析

客戶表示急單增加不少，但無法確定預估數據是否能穩定增加，不過允諾密切觀察。

Sandy：Thanks, Greg. But in such a case, I'll have to check with our planner to get a clearer answer. We also encountered a big surge in orders received from all over the world in the past few weeks. So far as I know, our production lines are full now and the situation will continue for at least 3 months.

謝謝你，Greg。不過若是這樣的話，我得和生管確認，才有辦法給你清楚的答案。在過去幾星期裡，我們全球各地訂單也是突然爆增。據我所理解，我們產線已滿檔，而且這情況還會持續至少三個月。

Greg：Good to hear that, but I hope it won't affect your delivery plans for our forecast. We'll need your commitment on punctual delivery of all our orders up to the present.

好消息是沒錯，但是希望不會影響我們預估訂單的交期。對於我們至今的訂單，你得承諾準時交貨。

客戶聽了開始擔心交期受影響，正常反應。

Sandy：We'll definitely do our utmost to keep the schedule unchanged, however I must say it will be really difficult, if not impossible. We're reviewing our master plan on a daily basis so that we'll be able to constantly keep all our customers in the loop.

我們絕對會盡最大努力維持交期。不過我必需聲明，實際上確實很困難，只差沒說不可能。我們每天都在盯著交貨計畫表，好讓所有客戶都能即時得到最新資訊。

Greg：Now you have made me nervous, and I have to remind you that we didn't expect any changes regardless of whatever had happened to you. Please bear in mind that this is the reason why we have been cooperating with you for the weekly forecast practice.

現在你讓我開始緊張起來了，我得提醒你，不管發生了什麼事，我們都不期待有任何改變。也請記住，這是我們會一直配合你們要求提供每週預估最主要的原因。

客戶再次強調不允許延後交期。

Sandy：I got your point. And actually we appreciate your efforts in this regard very much. I can assure you it will pay off. Meanwhile, I found from our EDI system that yesterday you made significant changes to your delivery forecast again.

我懂你的意思。事實上我們很感激你們這麼費心配合，我可以保證貴公司會得到回報的。另外，我從 EDI 系統上發現，昨天你們又大幅修改了出貨預估。

廠商也明白，也持續鼓勵客戶繼續配合 EDI 預估數據的做法。

Greg：Yes, I'm sorry for that, but we did encounter some problems with materials supply. We're working hard on the problem and hopefully things will go back to normal in a couple of months.

是的，真是抱歉。上游原料供應確實出了些問題，我們正努力解決當中，希望能在一、二個月中恢復正常。

Dr. Lee 解析

很巧，客戶在最近 EDI 中更改需求預估，但表示那只是短期現象。

Sandy：I see. Many of the changes forced us to delay the delivery. Fortunately, under such circumstances, it is very likely that we'll be able to accommodate those rush orders without disrupting too much of our master plan. Nevertheless, I have to emphasize that frequent modifications of your forecast will cause serious trouble to our operations.

我明白了。其中不少修正會使我們得延後交貨。還挺幸運，如此一來，我們有機會能將產能轉來應付這些急單，不至於大幅影響到整個排程計畫。不過，我得再強調，常修改預估數據，會嚴重影響我們工廠運作。

雖然因此廠商才能挪出產能解決客戶急單問題，但還是提醒客戶可能導致的後果。

Greg：I understand that, but fluctuations in business are inevitable. What we can do is to incorporate them in the weekly forecast as early as possible. Or do you have any better suggestions?

我了解。不過訂單的波動在所難免，我們能做的就是及早反應在每週預估數據當中。不然你們有更好的建議嗎？

Sandy：The existing weekly update runs pretty effectively and I don't intend to change it. However I'd appreciate it if you could send a reminder to us whenever you find something significantly deviating from your forecast. Is that OK with you?

目前這套每週更新預估數據的做法效果還相當不錯，我並不想做任何改變。如果你們在發現任何明顯的變異後能夠及時提醒我們，那就感激不盡了。這樣 OK 嗎？

Greg：Sure thing. I'll personally do it to make sure everything is in good order.

那當然。我會親自盯著數據，確保一切在掌控當中。

Sandy：Thanks a lot. Now let me sum up what we just discussed. First, regarding these urgent orders you just mentioned, we'll make sure to meet your requirements. Second, current weekly forecast update will be maintained and you'll send a reminder for the abnormal alterations. Please bear in mind that the next several weeks will be very critical to us.

多謝你了。我再把剛才的討論總結一下：首先關於你們的急單，我們會確保滿足你們的需求。其次，維持現行每週更新預估數據，貴公司會即時告知不正常變異，也請特別留意下面幾星期的情形，對我們尤其重要。

廠商作會議總結。這點在視訊會議特別重要。

Greg：Got it, and thanks very much for the summary.

沒錯，記住了。謝謝你的總結。

NOTE

❶**955 ATP：955 Available-To-Promise**的縮寫：「**955**保證即時供貨」意謂著**95%**的訂單需求量在接單**5**天之內出貨完畢。

❷**982 ATP：982 Available-To-Promise**的縮寫：「**982**保證即時供貨」意謂著**98%**的訂單需求量在接單**2**天之内出貨完畢。。

❸**scenario**：情節、情境

Gentlemen, now you can try to imagine the scenario of this happening based on Emma's description.

各位，現在你們可以根據 Emma 的描述去想像這事件當時的情景。

❹**order fulfillment**：訂單履行

Ava, we need to execute our order fulfillment system process in a more effective way.

Ava，我們得更有效地執行訂單履行系統流程。

❺**seek**：尋求、追求、找

Because of the incident, we tried to seek other sources for FPC supply.

由於這次事件，我們嘗試著尋找其它 FPC 的供應來源。

❻**client**：客戶、顧客

Oh come on, I've had plenty of clients to take care of already.

噢，拜託啦！我已經有夠多客戶要照顧了。

⑦ precise：準確的、精確的

Cathy, you have to be more precise in describing the case.

Cathy，你得更精確來敘述這個案子。

⑧ demand forecast：需求預估、訂單預估

Larry, you're supposed to complete the monthly demand forecast in an hour.

Larry，你得在一小時內完成月需求預估。

⑨ a lot more：很多、非常多

同 much more。

Although Art is a rookie sales guy, he received a lot more orders than any of his colleagues did last month.

雖然 Art 是位菜鳥業務，上個月他收到的訂單要比任一位同事還多。

⑩ apart from：除了、除開、除此之外

Apart from adding more testing machines, we started to use robots in material handling.

除了增加測試機台數量，我們開始使用機械手臂搬運物料。

⑪ aforementioned：前述的、前面提起的

Ethan, with regard to the aforementioned possible delay, I'll further confirm upon my return.

Ethan，關於前述可能的延遲，我會在回去之後立刻確認。

NOTE

⑫demanding：要求高的、要求嚴苛的

Both purchasing and planning are very demanding jobs in terms of patience.

就耐性而言，採購和生管都是要求高耐性的工作。

⑬lead time：前置時間

Stella, you must find ways to shorten the delivery lead time for this particular order.

Stella，你必須設法縮短這張訂單的交期。

⑭be due to：因為、由於

Glen, the delay was due to the cancellation of the inbound flight on which our shipment was booked.

Glen，延誤的原因是載運那批貨的進口航班被取消了。

⑮complexity：複雜性、複雜程度

We terminated the healthcare project because of its complexity.

由於複雜度太高，我們終止了這項健康醫療案。

⑯involved：涉及到的、相關聯的

Derek, I'm not in a position to confirm now as the money involved is too large.

Derek，由於牽涉的金額太大，我沒法現在就確認。

⑰accurate：精確的

Jack, we need a more accurate instrument for the experiment.

Jack，我們需要一台更精確的儀器來進行這項實驗。

⑱ **shorten**：縮短、減短

We were given instructions to shorten the aluminum fabricating time from 80 minutes to 64 minutes.

我們收到指示，將鋁材加工時間由 80 分鐘縮短至 64 分鐘。

⑲ **eventually**：最後、終於、終究

Eventually, our engineers fixed the temperature chamber in time.

我們工程師們終於及時修好這台溫控箱了。

⑳ **lead to**：導致、引起

Jason, the breakdown of our precision calibrator will surely lead to the delay of the shipments to Sun Steel.

Jason，我們精密校正儀的故障絕對會導致延後出貨給 Sun Steel。

㉑ **stable**：平穩的、穩定的

It is important to keep stable and long-term relationships with our class-A customers.

和我們 A 級客戶保持長期穩定關係很重要。

㉒ **benefit**：（動）使…受惠

Steven, I assure you that our EDI program will eventually benefit both of us.

Steven，我向你保證，我們的 EDI 作法將會使你我雙方都受惠。

NOTE

㉓video conference：視訊會議

Charles, please join our video conference with Max's team tomorrow morning.

Charles，請你明天上午與我一起和 Max 團隊開視訊會議。

㉔update：更新

Grace, please make sure to send me your weekly market update tomorrow morning.

Grace，請務必在明天上午把你的每週市場更新訊息傳給我。

㉕couple of weeks：二星期，或是二星期再多一、二天

同 a couple of weeks。

Helen, the shipment will arrive in a couple of weeks.

Helen，那筆貨會在二星期內運到。

㉖wonder：（動）懷疑、想知道

Hey guys, I wonder if we're able to finish all the packaging tonight.

各位，我在想今晚我們到底能不能完成所有封裝工作。

㉗last：（動）持續

Allen, the bad news is that dock labor strike will begin later tonight and will last for 24 hours, same as last time.

Allen，壞消息是碼頭工人今晚即將開始為期 24 小時的罷工，就像上次那樣。

28 rush orders：急單、緊急訂單

We're all working three shifts on those rush orders in order to meet the demanding deadline.

為了這些急單，我們全員三班工作以便能趕上嚴苛的交貨期限。

29 premature：過早的、尚未準備好的

It is premature now to say the system will fail to meet our expectation.

要現在就說這套系統沒法達到我們的預期，時機還太早。

說明：不要把 premature 與 immature 混爲一談了。Immature 是不成熟的或發展不完全的。

The software is immature, so it is too early to say if the system will meet our expectations or not.

軟體尚未開發完全，因此要下斷語說這套系統是否會達到我們的期望還太早。

30 at the moment：此時、此刻、現在、當下

At the moment, our production engineers don't have a feasible solution to the problem.

此時此刻，我們的製造工程師並沒有一套可行的解決方法。

31 tell：分辨、斷定

It's hard to tell if the system will work.

很難斷定這制度是否能行得通。

NOTE

㉜ **steady**：穩定的、平穩的

Ruth, we see a steady upward trend in the demand of our AT series.

Ruth，對於我們 AT 系列的需求，我們看出一股穩定向上的趨勢。

㉝ **keep you closely informed**：讓你知道最新情況

Ian, you stay focused on the project and we'll keep you closely informed.

Ian，專心在你的案子上，我們會隨時讓你了解情況的。

㉞ **encounter**：遭遇、遇見

We encountered tremendous difficulties while testing these smart sensors.

當我們在測試這些智慧型感應器時，遭遇到極大的困難。

㉟ **surge**：激增

A surge of orders in recent weeks has kept us on our toes.

近幾星期來激增的訂單可真把我們忙壞了。

註：keep us on our toes 使我們忙碌起來。

㊱ **so far as I know**：據我所知

No worries, Becky. As far as I know, the new testing machine will arrive this afternoon.

別擔心，Becky。據我所知，新的測試機下午就會運到。

NOTE

㊲ punctual：準時的

Punctual delivery is crucial to many of the industries.

準時交貨對許多產業來說至關重要。

㊳ up to the present：直到目前為止

Up to the present, we haven't received any response from the freight forwarder.

直到目前為止，我們還沒得到貨運代理公司任何回應。

㊴ do our utmost：盡最大努力

也可說 do our best。

Lydia, we will do our utmost to accelerate your order by two days.

Lydia，我們會盡最大努力提前兩天交貨。

㊵ on a daily basis：按照每天

In order to provide accurate data, we review our master plan on a daily basis.

為了提供準確的數據，我們每天檢討排程主檔。

㊶ constantly：時時地、經常地、不斷地

While I was traveling, I constantly checked my email so as not to miss any important messages.

我在旅行當中，也常常檢查 email，以防遺漏任何重要訊息。

NOTE

42 keep…in the loop：讓…知道最新情況、讓…保留在決策過程中

也可說 keep…closely informed。

Carl, please make sure to keep Sandra in the loop.

Carl，請務必讓 Sandra 隨時了解狀況。

43 nervous：緊張、焦慮不安

The late arrival of the PCBs made Tony so nervous.

PCB 的延後運到，讓 Tony 焦慮不已。

44 regardless of：不論、不管、無論

We will not sign the agreement regardless of what we have orally agreed to do.

不管曾經口頭答應過什麼，我們就是不簽這份合約。

45 bear in mind：記住、牢記

Nathan, please bear in mind that Rex asked us to finish testing the new oven by 8:00 tonight.

Nathan 請記住，Rex 要求我們在今晚 8:00 之前完成那台新烤箱的測試。

46 in this regard：在這方面、關於此事

In this regard, we don't have any clue.

關於這點，我們不清楚到底是怎麼一回事。

47 **assure**：向…保證、使…放心

Bob, I can assure you that we'll deliver on time.

Bob，我能向你保證，我們會準時交貨。

48 **pay off**：有成功結果、得到利益

Thank God, Jacob. Your effort paid off.

感謝神啊 Jacob，你的努力成功了！

49 **EDI system**：電子數據交換系統，為**Electronic Data Interchange** 的縮寫。

50 **go back to normal**：回復正常

The production went back to normal after the engineers fixed the hydraulic system.

在工程師修好液壓系統後，生產就回復正常了。

51 **force**：（動）迫使、逼迫

The sudden layoff forces me to think deeper into the future.

突然的被解雇，迫使我更深層的去思考未來。

52 **fortunately**：幸運地、幸好

Fortunately, the floods didn't do too much damage to our factory.

幸好水災並沒帶給廠房多大的災害。

NOTE

53 very likely：很有可能

We will start to test the new bonding machines, very likely from next Monday.

我們很可能從下周一就開始測試新焊接機。

54 accommodate：容納、接納、提供

Cathy, we will surely try our best to accommodate all your requirements.

Cathy，我們一定會盡最大努力滿足你們所有需求。

55 disrupt：擾亂、使中斷

The unexpected breakdown of the oven disrupted our experiment.

烤箱意外的故障，中斷了我們的實驗。

56 nevertheless：然而、儘管如此

Eric, I fully understand your position. Nevertheless, you still have to finish it on time.

Eric，我完全理解你的處境。儘管如此，你還是得準時完成工作。

57 emphasize：強調

I can't emphasize enough the importance of product quality.

產品品質的重要性永遠強調不完。

58 frequent：時常發生的、頻繁的

As a frequent flyer, I'm used to jet lag.

身為航空公司常客，我已習慣時差了。

59 **modification**：修改、修正

Olivia, please show me the modifications against the previous version.

Olivia，請對照先前版本，讓我看看修改的地方。

60 **cause trouble**：引起麻煩、帶來麻煩

Mark, your frequent tardiness to work has caused a lot of trouble for us.

Mark，你上班經常遲到已經帶給我們很大的麻煩。

61 **fluctuation**：上下波動、起伏變動

We've seen fluctuations in our export business for a long time.

我們在過去一段長時間裡，看到出口生意起起伏伏。

62 **inevitable**：不可避免的

Even with the Six Sigma system in place, errors are still inevitable.

即使實施 Six Sigma 制度，錯誤還是無法避免。

63 **incorporate**：包含、併入、合併

Kim, we will incorporate your proposition into our sales strategy.

Kim，我們會將你的提議併入我們的銷售策略裡。

NOTE

64 existing：現存的、現有的

According to the existing purchasing policy, we must have quotations from at least three different vendors.

根據公司現有的採購政策，我們至少要收到三家以上的報價單。

65 intend to：打算、想要

Jeremy, I don't intend to be picky, but you're wrong about this.

Jeremy，我不是想挑剔，可是這點你錯了。

66 reminder：提醒、提示

We received a reminder from Janet of the coming price hike.

我們收到 Janet 發來的一個即將漲價的提醒。

67 whenever：隨時、無論何時、每當

Believe it or not, whenever we're busy with rush orders, there's a blackout.

你相信嗎？每當我們在忙急單，就會斷電。

68 deviate：偏離

Morris, what you just said deviates from the conclusions we agreed upon at the meeting last week.

Morris，你剛剛所說的，已經偏離了上星期會議中我們達成的共識。

69 sure thing：當然、一定、沒問題，非常口語的說法。

Daniel, can you give me a ride to the station? Daniel: Sure thing.

Daniel，能給個便車去車站嗎？Daniel：當然可以呀！

sure thing 也有非口語的說法：

We gave them the a top quality product at the best price and the best delivery, so winning the order was a sure thing.

我們用最好的價格和最棒的交期，提供給他們一個頂級品質的產品。如此贏得訂單，是理所當然。

70 in good order：妥當、就緒、有條理

Allison, please make sure everything is in good order.

Allison，請務必確保一切都準備妥當了。

71 sum up：做結論、總結

Randy, you may want to sum up now for today's meeting.

Randy，你現在可以替今天會議做總結了。

72 abnormal：不正常的、反常的

I was shocked by his abnormal behavior in the office this morning.

我被他今早在辦公室裡的反常行為嚇了一跳。

73 alteration：更改、改變

Monica, please keep me informed of any alterations made in the meeting.

Monica，請務必讓我知道在會議中所做的任何更動。

NOTE

74 critical：關鍵的、極重要的

Customer service has become one of the most critical factors in winning orders.

客服已經成為諸多贏得訂單最重要的因素之一。

75 got it：（平述句）我懂了，是一種非常口語的回答方式，甚至在文法上是錯誤的。

不過平日在口語上使用無傷大雅，正確說法是 I've got it.

Lesson 5 品質管理制度 Quality Management System

課文重點① Summary 1

An effective Quality Management System (QMS) has become a much more important evaluation criteria when selecting suppliers. The QMS includes the quality assurance system and the quality control system. Basically, customers tend to care more about the methods and tools adopted by the system. There are quite a few QC methods such as control charts, sampling inspection, and life testing. With regard to quality improvement tools, 8D and 6 Sigma are more popular than others such as Brainstorming and Design of Experiment.

一套有效的品質管理制度，已成為現今供應商評核過程中極為重要的指標之一。品質管理制度涵蓋品保制度及品管制度。除開產品品質本身，實際上 B2B 客戶多半會想了解廠商品管（QC）與品保（QA）方法和工具。品管方法長久以來多半沿用管制圖、抽樣檢驗、或壽命測試。而品保制度中的品質改善工具則持續演進，現今廣被電子業採用的 8D 和 6 Sigma 就比腦力激盪和實驗設計更常被使用。

品管、品保手法 QC、QA tools

Sandra : **Procurement Manager, Parker Electronics (Taiwan Branch)** 採購經理

Michael : **Sales Manager, Device Technology (Taiwan)** 業務經理

Janet : **VP Quality, Device Technology (Taiwan)** 品質副總

Sandra is visiting Sandra 前來拜訪

Michael : Welcome, Sandra. It's so nice to have you here at our plant. Per your earlier request, we will cover both the QC and the QA functions in the meeting. This is Janet, our Quality VP. She's responsible for the overall quality management of our company.

Sandra，歡迎蒞臨。很高興你能來我們工廠。根據你先前的要求，在會議中我們會討論品管和品保。這位是 Janet，我們的品質副總。Janet 負責我們公司的整體品質管理。

Janet : Hi Sandra, so nice to meet you. This must be your first time visiting us.

嗨 Sandra，很高興見到你。這一定是你頭一次來我們公司吧。

Sandra : So nice to meet you too. Yes, this is the first time. And thanks for arranging the meeting. Firstly, I need to know how quality control is being implemented in your factory.

彼此彼此。沒錯，我是頭一次來，謝謝你們的安排。首先我想了解你們的品管制度。

Michael：Before I introduce our QC system, I'd like to emphasize that our overall quality strategy is based on the TQM concept. TQM stands for Total Quality Management. It is a concept of developing the organizational quality culture by adopting an across-the-board QA and QC network and procedures.

在介紹我們品管制度前，我想強調我們品質策略的基礎是 TQM 的概念。TQM 就是全面品質管理，也是一個藉由全面採用品保與品管網路和流程，建立起公司品質文化的概念。

Sandra：I see. It sounds familiar to me as we also adopt TQM in our company.

我懂。我還挺熟悉這些，因為我們公司也是採用 TQM。

Michael：Glad to hear that. OK, I'll start with the QC system. Firstly, we have a quality department reporting direct to the CEO with a major responsibility of conducting Incoming QC, In-process QC, and the Final QC.

真高興聽你這麼說。好，我就從 QC 制度開始，首先介紹組織。我們的品質部門直接向執行長報告，主要負責進料檢驗、製程品管、和成品品管。

Sandra：Good, how about the seven basic quality tools? Are you using them all?

好，那品管 7 大手法呢？你們都有用上嗎？

Michael：I was about to explain this to you. Among the seven tools, we're using four only, namely Cause-and-Effect Diagram, we call it the Fishbone Diagram, Check Sheet, Pareto Chart, and Control Chart. We want to keep the system simple, but effective.

我才正準備要向你說明呢！七大手法中我們只用了四種，要因分析圖法，我們稱做魚骨圖法、檢查表法、柏拉圖法、和管制圖法。我們想讓系統更簡單有效。

Sandra: Great ! I believe you must have a well-managed production line, probably a more automated line, isn't it?
太好了！我相信你們產線一定管理得很好，可能是自動化較高的產線，對不對？

Michael: You're right, and for a procurement person, you're very good with QC subjects. How come?
沒錯。以一位採購來說，你對品管很內行，是什麼原因呢？

Sandra: Thanks. Actually I had worked in the QC function for two years before being transferred to the purchasing department. Now, how about the quality improvement tools?
謝謝誇獎。實際上，在調來採購部門以前，我曾在品管單位服務過二年。接下來，你們品質改善制度又是如何。

Michael: No wonder you're so familiar with all of this. OK, about the quality improvement tools, apart from those mentioned before, we're using mainly SPC, 6 Sigma, and Ford 8D.
難怪你對這些那麼熟悉。好，關於品質改善工具，除了上述那些之外，我們主要用統計製程管制 SPC、 6 Sigma、和福特 8D。

Sandra: They are all the mainstream of contemporary quality improvement tools. I'd like to know more about the 6 Sigma.
這些都是當今品質改善主流工具，我想多了解一些 6 Sigma。

Michael: I'll do my best, though I'm not an expert on this. Basically 6 Sigma serves to improve, design and redesign, and manage the process. In other words, 6 Sigma assures the correct process from the beginning to the end on a continuous basis.

雖然我不是 6 Sigma 專家，不過我會盡力說明給你聽。基本上，6 Sigma 是為了改善、設計與重新設計、和管理整個製程。換句話說，6 Sigma 從頭到尾持續保證製程品質。

Sandra：That's good enough, thanks very much. If we need to know more, our quality engineers will start establishing a dialogue directly with Janet. Is it OK with you, Janet?

這樣已經夠好了，謝謝。如果我們想多了解，我們的品質工程師會和 Janet 建立直接對話機制。可以嗎，Janet？

Janet：Sure thing. We'll be glad to do it.

當然可以，我們很樂意那麼做。

Michael：Awesome! Now I'm going to introduce our product warranty policy. I believe you also have a concern about this.

太好了，現在我來說明產品保固政策，相信你也很關心保固。

Sandra：Yes, I do, because I have to deal with it on a daily basis. What is your product warranty?

是的，因為我每天都得要處理保固問題。你們的產品保固如何？

Michael：For our standard products, it's one year from invoice date. There are exceptions for a few on-demand special cases though, and I'd also like to tell you how we handle returns.

我們標準品是由發票日期後提供一年保固，是有些因應客戶請求的特殊案例。我也來說明退貨處理原則。

Sandra：Oh yes, that's really important. From time to time I was confused by the different requirements laid down by different companies.

對，那真的很重要。我經常被不同廠商的不同要求弄昏頭了。

Michael: I believe we have a pretty standardized procedure. If a return is under warranty and was only subjected to normal usage, we will replace it with a new one. We'll handle the case with an 8D problem solving process.

相信我們的還算是標準程序。如果還在保固期限內而且是屬於正常使用損壞，我們會換新品給你們，也會用 8D 來處理退貨案子。

Sandra: Would you please elaborate on "normal usage"?

可以請你詳細解釋「正常使用」嗎？

Michael: It means the damage was caused only by the problems of the materials or the manufacturing of the product. In other words, any damage outside of natural causes are not warranted. Neither are human errors on your or your customers' side.

所謂正常使用，表示損壞原因是由於材料或生產工藝不良所造成。換句話說，任何非自然原因造成的損壞，我們是不保固的。若是人為失誤，無論是貴司的或是貴司客戶的，也都不保固。

Sandra: OK, I understand, but this could be a grey area, so we'll see.

好，我明白了。這可能會是個灰色地帶，以後再說吧。

Michael: And you'll need to get an RMA number from us before you send the damaged parts back to us.

不過在送回不良品之前，你們得拿到我們的 RMA 號碼。

Sandra: I hope we won't have to use it too frequently in the future.

希望以後不需經常使用到 RMA 啦。

1 **evaluation**：評估、評核

Leo, please be sure to attend the technical evaluation meeting tomorrow morning.

Leo，請務必參加明天上午的技術評估會議。

2 **criteria**：標準、指標、條件

Felix, B/B ratio is only one of the many criteria we take into consideration for a promotion.

Felix，B/B 值只是我們決定升遷的考慮條件之一。

說明：B/B ratio 是 book-to-bill ratio 的縮寫，指「接單出貨比」。

3 **care**：在意、關心

Bess, what we care the most about is whether you're capable enough for the job.

Bess，我們最在意的，是你能否勝任這份工作。

4 **adopt**：採用、採納

We're adopting 6 Sigma quality improvement tools, even for the R&D operations.

即便是研發工作，我們都採用 6 Sigma 品質改善工具。

5 **quite a few**：很多

等同 many。

Quite a few of us have obtained the ASQ Certification.

我們很多人都持有 ASQ 證照。

NOTE

⑥control charts：管制圖

Control charts are widely used in the quality control of manufacturing processes.

製程品管中經常使用管制圖。

⑦sampling inspection：抽樣檢驗

Sampling inspection is one of the most popular inspection methods used by mass-production manufacturers.

抽樣檢驗是大規模生產製造商最常使用的檢驗方法之一。

⑧life testing：壽命測試

In the consumer electronics industry, life testing is a popular QC tool.

消費性電子業經常使用壽命測試作為品管工具。

⑨with regard to：關於、有關

With regard to upgrading our QA effectiveness, we've invested enormously in reinforcing our quality system.

關於提升品保成效，我們已經巨額投資在強化品質制度上。

⑩improvement：改善、改進

Eli, I want to see immediate improvement on the yield of our high end products.

Eli，我要求立即改善我們高階產品良率。

⑪8D：**8D**問題解決程序，為**8D Problem Solving Process**簡寫。

⑫ **6 Sigma**：6 Sigma（製程改善工具）

⑬ **popular**：流行的、受歡迎的、通俗的

The 6 Sigma is a popular quality improvement tool in today's manufacturing industry.

當今製造業裡，6 Sigma 是一種很流行的品質改善工具。

⑭ **Brainstorming**：腦力激盪（製程改善工具）

⑮ **Design of Experiment**：實驗設計（製程改善工具）

⑯ **procurement**：採購

Delia has been with our procurement department for more than 10 years.

Delia 已經在我們採購部門服務超過 10 年了。

⑰ **per somebody's request**：根據某人的要求

Per Ivy's request, I've scheduled a conference call for a global supply chain review meeting the day after tomorrow.

根據 Ivy 的要求，我安排好了在後天召開全球供應鏈檢討電話會議。

⑱ **cover**：包括、涵蓋

The meeting agenda also covers the technical issues you mentioned last week.

會議事項也包括你上週所提到的技術議題。

NOTE

⑲ **overall**：整體的

The overall performance of our team turned out to be quite satisfactory.

我們團隊整體表現相當令人滿意。

⑳ **arrange**：安排

Paula, would you please arrange a video conference among all QC teams for tomorrow afternoon.

Paula，能請你安排明天下午開全體品管團隊視訊會議嗎？

㉑ **implement**：實施、執行

Starting next Monday, we will implement a weekly planning & reporting system.

從下周一開始，我們會實施一種週計畫報告制度。

㉒ **I'd like to**：我想要

I would like to 的縮寫，語意比 I want to 婉轉。

I'd like to take a break now.

我現在想休息一下。

㉓ **emphasize**：強調

Dora, I'd like to emphasize the importance of being considerate to others.

Dora，我想要強調體諒他人的重要性。

24 be based on：根據、基於、以…為基礎

Gary, the percentage of the salary adjustment is based on your Q4 performance evaluation.

Gary，調薪百分比是根據你 Q4 的績效評核。

25 TQM：全面品質管理，為**Total Quality Management** 的縮寫。

26 concept：觀念、概念

Helen, we just explained the concept of teamwork.

Helen，我們剛才解釋了團隊合作的概念。

27 stands for：代表、意味著

The buzzer sound stands for abnormal surface temperature.

蜂鳴器聲響意味著表面溫度不正常。

28 culture：文化

Adapting to a different business culture is by no means an easy task.

要適應一個不同的企業文化絕非一件容易事。

29 across-the-board：全面性的

There's a notice of an across-the-board hiring freeze with immediate effect.

有一張即刻生效的全面人事凍結通告。

NOTE

㉚ **network**：網路

We're going to install a centralized manufacturing network for all production lines next week.

我們下星期將為所有產線安裝一套集中式製造網路。

㉛ **procedure**：程序、過程

Gilbert, I know it sounds weird, but we have to follow the procedures.

Gilbert，我知道這聽起來很怪，但是我們得依照程序走。

㉜ **it sounds familiar**：聽起來很熟悉（經常聽到的意思）

Maggie, does it sound familiar that we're short of capacity again?

Maggie，我們產能又不夠了，聽起來很熟悉是吧？

㉝ **conduct**：實施、執行

QA department conducted a 2-day ISO 9001 internal audit last week.

上星期品保部門實施了一次為期二天的 ISO 9001 內部稽核。

㉞ **Incoming QC**：進料品管

㉟ **In-process QC**：製程品管

㊱ **Final QC**：成品品管

37 be about to：即將、正要（做動作）

I was about to hit the road when Iris called.

當 Iris 打來電話時，我正準備上路。

38 Cause-and-Effect Diagram：要因分析圖

39 Fishbone Diagram：魚骨圖

也稱作 Ishikawa diagram 石川圖。

40 Check Sheet：檢查表

41 Pareto Chart：柏拉圖

42 Control Chart：管制圖

43 well-managed：管理良好的

A well-managed customer service operation makes great contributions to the company.

一個管理良好的客服作業能帶給公司極大的貢獻。

44 probably：可能、或許、大概

Daisy, I was told that the samples would probably arrive sometime in the afternoon.

Daisy，我知道樣品可能會在下午運到。

45 automated：自動的、自動化的

The automated sorting machines increased our total output by 25%.

這些自動分選機使我們總產出增加 25%。

NOTE

46 How come?：為何、為什麼、怎麼會

Miles, how come your desk is always in such a mess?

Miles，你的桌子為什麼老是這麼亂？

47 transfer：轉移、調任

I'll be officially transferred to the supply chain department on July 1.

我將在 7 月 1 日正式調到供應鏈部門。

48 no wonder：難怪、怪不得

No wonder we have such a high yield.

難怪我們良率這麼高。

49 familiar with：對…熟悉

Everybody except Samuel is familiar with the procedures.

除了 Samuel 以外，大家都很熟悉這程序。

50 apart from：除開、除了以外

Mark, apart from calibrating the system, you need to finish installing two new systems by midnight.

Mark，你除了校正好這系統，在午夜前，還得安裝好二套新系統。

51 mainly：主要地

I'll be focusing mainly on developing new channel business in the coming two weeks.

下來二週裡，我主要會專注在新通路生意的開發。

52 **mainstream**：主流

The ultra-high temperature thermometers have been the mainstream of our product portfolio.

超高溫度儀一直都是我們產品組合中的主流。

53 **contemporary**：現代的、當代的

SPC is a popular quality improvement tool based on contemporary statistical models.

以當代統計模式為基礎的統計製程管制，是一種廣泛被採用的品質改善工具。

54 **serve to**：用來

The grading system serves to substantially speed up the food processing.

這套分級系統用來大幅加快食品加工速度。

55 **assure**：保證、使放心

Bob, I can assure you that the shipment will arrive on time.

Bob，我向你保證準時到貨。

56 **correct**：正確的

You're correct in saying that I was indeed upset.

你說的沒錯，我確實很不開心。

NOTE

57 continuous：連續的、持續的

We are making continuous progress on reducing our manufacturing cost.

我們持續在降低製造成本上獲得進展。

58 start：練習

start 的二種句型：

Andrew started taking quality-related courses two weeks ago.

Andrew 從二星期前開始上品質相關的課程。

Amy wasted no time and started to prepare the QA presentation.

Amy 立即開始準備品保簡報。

59 establish：建立

Felix has done a great job establishing solid vendor relationships.

Felix 在建立穩固供應商關係上表現的真好。

60 dialogue：對話

I'm having a more frequent dialogue with Janet than ever before.

現階段我和 Janet 之間的對話比從前頻繁多了。

61 Is it OK with you?：這樣你可以嗎？這樣你能同意嗎？這樣你能接受嗎？

62 sure thing：沒問題、當然可以

Jason, can I borrow your meter for a minute? Sure thing, Eric.

Jason，你電表借用一下好嗎？沒問題，Eric！

63 product warranty：產品保固

We are offering an 18-month product warranty for all of our standard products.

對於我們所有的標準品，我們提供 18 個月產品保固。

64 concern：關心、擔心

I'm concerned about the deteriorating quality of your high-end products.

我對你們高階產品品質日益低落感到憂心。

65 on a daily basis：每天，指每天都發生

I'm following up with my sales reps via the CRM system on a daily basis.

我每天藉由 CRM 系統和我手下的業務人員保持聯繫。

66 invoice date：開發票日

Lillian, make sure to pay our suppliers according to the invoice date.

Lillian，請務必根據發票日期付款給供應廠商。

NOTE

67 exception：例外

We always shipped within 24 hours after receiving payment, with only a few exceptions.

除了少數例外，我們都在收到貨款後 24 小時內出貨。

68 a few：幾個、一些

We received only a few complaints concerning product quality in the past 2 months.

在過去二個月裡，我們只收到幾次產品品質客訴。

69 on-demand：由客戶提出要求的

We offer our customers an output matching service on demand.

若客戶提出要求，我們會提供輸出匹配服務。

70 though：雖然、儘管、不過

No worries. We'll figure it out, a bit late though.

別擔心，我們會想出辦法，只不過會遲些。

71 from time to time：有時、不時、偶而

From time to time, we ran into some trouble and got stuck.

偶而我們會碰上麻煩，動彈不得。

72 confuse：迷惑、混淆

Vincent was confused by the weird data collected from the test instrument.

Vincent 對測試儀器所收集到的數據感到困惑。

73 lay down：制定、規定

A strict inspection procedure was laid down by our quality department for all outsourced parts.

針對所有外製零件，我們品質部門制定了一套嚴格的檢驗程序。

74 standardized：標準化的

All the shipping and receiving procedures were standardized.

所有收發程序都已經標準化了。

75 under warranty：在保固期中

I'm sorry, sir. It's not under warranty any more.

先生，對不起，這已不在保固期限裡了。

76 normal usage：正常使用

I'm sorry, Dale. Apparently the unit wasn't under normal usage. The PCB had been totally burned.

Dale，很抱歉，這顯然不是在正常使用狀態下損壞的，主機板已經完全燒壞了。

說明：多數產業將「正常使用狀態」定義爲「非人爲疏失或非天然災害」，或將「正常使用狀態下損壞」狹義定義成「由於材料本身或組裝工藝問題導致產品損壞」。

77 replace：替換、更換

Michael, the oil seal of the No. 3 tester needs to be replaced.

Michael，3 號測試機的油封得換新了。

NOTE

78 8D problem solving process：8D問題解決程序

The 8D problem solving process is being widely employed by many industries.

時下很多產業廣泛使用 8D 問題解決程序。

79 elaborate：闡述、詳細說明

Nancy, please elaborate on the 6 Sigma.

Nancy，你詳細解釋 6 Sigma。

80 in other words：換言之

In other words, Matt, you'd better finish coding before Ted loses his head.

Matt，換句話說，你最好在 Ted 發飆前把程式寫好。

81 natural causes：自然因素

Dan, by natural causes we mean under normal usage.

Dan，所謂自然因素，是指在正常使用狀態下。

82 human error：人為過失、人為疏失

Eric, you must realize a human error like this will cause serious damage to the company.

Eric，你必須了解，像這樣的人為疏失會帶給公司嚴重傷害。

83 grey area：灰色地帶

You got to know, Ryan. It's good or failed. There's no grey area.

Ryan，你必須了解，要嘛合格，否則就是不合格，中間沒有灰色地帶。

84 **we'll see**：到時後就知道了，常用於口語。

I'm not sure if it will work. We'll see.

我沒把握那能行得通，到時後就知道了。

85 **RMA number**：退貨授權號碼

Be sure to get an RMA number from us prior to sending the unit back to us.

寄回給我們之前，請務必向我們要一組退貨授權號碼。

課文重點② Summary 2

Project management has been gaining popularity in recent years as a result of its effectiveness in assuring business success. A typical project manager works under tremendous pressures from different aspects of the project, such as resource, cost, quality, schedule, satisfaction, and scope. In some cases, project managers are being held responsible for the successful product launch and the overall performance of the project. Project managers work with both external partners like component vendors and internal co-workers such as R&D engineers, the supply chain team, and the marketing team. As a consequence, the day-to-day communications and co-ordination usually takes up the majority of their working hours. In a B2B business mode, project managers are rewarded by the successful closing of a project. By contrast, a collaborating partner, such as a component vendor, is rewarded by the award of the purchase order from the project owner.

由於專案管理在當今產業中實施成效顯著，專案管理技術也愈加快速受到重視。一位典型專案經理經常得承受來自不同商業面相，如資源、成本、時程、品質、範圍、和滿意度的壓力。某些情況下，專案經理除了負責專案順利推出外，還得擔起最終績效的重責。專案經理既得對外也得對內，對外包括與配合的供應商合作，對內則要與公司內部同事如研發工程師、供應鏈團隊、和行銷團隊共事。也因此，專案經理的工作內容多在進行溝通協調。在 B2B 模式中，專案經理的績效由執行結果來決定；相對來說，供應廠商等協作廠商就由獲得訂單得到肯定和獎勵。

專案經理與業務 PM & Sales

Emma：**Project Manager, Abbot Inc. (U.S.A.)** 產品經理

Glenn：**Senior Product Manager, Abbot Inc. (U.S.A.)** 資深產品經理

Neil：**Sales Manager, Zenith Tech (Taiwan)** 業務經理

Neil initiates the conference call Neil 開啓多方電話會議

Emma：Hi Neil, the second time this week. What's so urgent? I can smell your anxiety.

嗨 Neil，這禮拜你第二次找我了，什麼事這麼緊急啊？我都能聞出你的焦慮。

業務總是急於知道是否拿到專案訂單（design-win）。

Neil：Yes, Emma. I really need your help regarding Project Cougar.

是啊 Emma，關於 Cougar 專案，我真的需要你幫忙。

看起來與 PM 關係相當不錯。

: OK, but you just sent me the samples three days ago. We are still testing them on our machines.
好，可是你三天前才送樣給我，現在都還在機器上測試呢！

測試還是得看研發工程師的進度。

: Oh is that so? Can you speed up a little bit, please? Sorry, I don't mean to press you, however my boss has been pushing me real hard.
是這樣啊？能趕緊測完嗎？拜託啦！抱歉，我不是要給你壓力，不過我老闆一直在催我。

業務責任在身還是得請 PM 幫忙催進度。

: Please believe me that I've done all I can to push for the results. You should know how much time it takes to complete all the tests.
要相信我啦！已經盡力在催了，你該知道測試得花多久時間的。

溝通是 PM 強項。

Neil：Thanks. Then how much time will it take for you to receive the results from your engineers?

謝謝啦，你估計還得多久才能從工程師那裏拿到測試結果？

Emma：It will take another week, I guess. I'll try harder to shorten it, OK?

我估計還得一星期。我會努力再縮短些，好嗎？

Neil：Appreciate it. How about Project Crocodile? It has been almost a month since you approved our samples.

真感謝你。那 Crocodile 專案現在如何？從承認我們樣機到現在都快一個月了。

Emma：We still have to wait for the final BOM from our R&D department. They've been too busy to do it, I guess. I'll check with them later today.

我還在等研發部把料表搞定後交給我。我猜他們是太忙才會如此吧，今天稍晚我再問他們好了。

PM 告知進度，也答應再追蹤。

Neil：Thanks very much. By the way, you told me last Friday that you're planning an audit trip to Taipei. Have you finalized the trip plan?

多謝。對了，上週五你說要來一趟台北作稽核，行程決定了嗎？

業務跟著詢問 PM 原訂專案稽核行程，稽核是大事。

Emma：I didn't have the time to send you all the details, but I know that the audit is scheduled on July 15 for Project Buffalo at Hsinchu. I am looking to arrive on July 14 and depart on July 16. You may want to check if the schedule suits your team, and confirm later on.

我還沒有時間把所有細節傳給你，不過我知道 Buffalo 專案的稽核是排定 7 月 15 號在新竹廠。我預計 7 月 14 號到台灣， 7 月 16 號回美國。你查一下並確認這樣行程可以嗎。

Neil：No problem with us. I just checked into my calendar.

沒問題，我剛剛查過行事曆。

Emma：Good. I'll send you all the details tomorrow morning. Oh, my boss Glenn, just joined. Glenn, it's Neil from Zenith Tech.

好，明天早上我會傳細節給你。噢，我老闆 Glenn 剛剛加入會議。

此時大 PM Glenn 加入電話會議。

Glenn：Hi Neil, how's it going? I need to discuss a few things with you.

嗨 Neil，你好嗎？有幾件事我得和你討論。

顯然有要事討論。

Neil：Hi Glenn, it could've been worse. I've been under tremendous pressure, mostly from Emma's projects. I hope you will bring me some good news.

嗨 Glenn，我還好。近來壓力很大，多半是因為 Emma 的案子。希望你帶來些好消息。

業務趁機給壓力。

Glenn：Well, both good and bad. Firstly, it is about Project Mars that we completed last November and launched on Jan 5 this year. The project turned out to be not too successful because of a couple of mishaps, partly from your end. Here's a report from the post-mortem meeting we held yesterday. Please hand it over to Todd when he comes back from vacation. We'd expect him to respond within two weeks.

呃，好消息壞消息都有。首先是關於去年 11 月完成，今年 1 月 5 日推出的 Mars 專案，受到過程中一些事故影響，其中一部份是由你們所引起，導致 Mars 不能算是成功。這裡有一份我們昨天開過的案後檢討（post-mortem）報告，請你在 Todd 休假回來交給他，我們希望他能在二星期內做回應。

不愧是大 PM，掌握主導權。先給案後檢討（post-mortem）報告，要求業務帶回給主管並要求回覆。

Neil：No problem. I'll make sure he does it in time.
沒問題。我會確保他即時回覆。

Glenn：Good. Emma, you may want to tell him the good news now.
好。Emma 你現在可以告訴他好消息了。

大 PM 鬆口請手下透露好消息給業務。

Emma：Oh yes! Good news, Neil. Regarding Project Lynx, we'll be awarding 75% of the RF Module business to you. We just made that decision shortly before we started the conference call. Our supply chain team will provide you with splits by month through our normal forecasts.
對啊！Neil，好消息喔！關於 Lynx 專案，我們會給你們 75% RF 模組訂單，在剛剛會議開始前我們才做決定的。我們供應鏈團隊會透過平日預估，提供你們按月所需的數據。

PM 告知將下單，也確認配額比重。

Neil：Thanks so much. Now I can sit back and relax a little bit. And cheers!

謝謝啦。我現在可以比較舒服坐著鬆口氣了。來，敬你們，乾杯！

Emma：Hold on, Neil. There's more for you. We'll be sending you an RFP, very likely tomorrow morning, for Project Bison. It is our most important project in the second half of the year.

Neil 等等，還有更多好消息要給你啊！我們很可能會在明天傳 Bison 專案的 RFP 給你，那是我們下半年最重要的專案。

PM 表示還有好消息，將發出新案 RFP。

Neil：Hey Emma, is this real? I didn't expect we'd have so much to talk about during this conference call at all. And you didn't even mention Project Bison to me until now. I guess God knows what I really need for the upcoming performance review. Thank you so much .

喂 Emma，是真的嗎？我完全沒預期在這會議上談這麼多。而且你一直到現在才提起這 Bison 專案。我猜是因為上帝知道我真的需要這些業績來面對即將到來的績效評核吧！謝謝二位啦！

業務喜出望外，連忙表示這是雪中送炭。

Emma：No problem. We'll send you the details by mail tomorrow. Now cheers!

沒問題，小事一樁。明天我們會把詳細資料寄給你。來，乾杯！

完美收場。

❶ **project management**：專案管理

❷ **gain**：贏得、取得

Josh failed to gain Brandon's trust, even if he tried so hard.

既使 Josh 很努力想得到 Brandon 的信任，卻還是失敗了。

❸ **popularity**：普及、流行

Jazz started to gain popularity in many Asian cities.

爵士樂在許多亞洲城市中開始流行了。

❹ **as a result of**：由於

As a result of the material shortage, we had to pay a premium to get the quantity we required.

由於原料短缺，我們付了高價才買到我們所需要的數量。

NOTE

⑤ effectiveness：效果、效用

The effectiveness of the program was largely determined by the design of the system.

方案是否有效多半取決於系統設計。

⑥ typical：典型的、代表性的

Dylan is a typical sales guy, as he knows little but talks too much.

Dylan 是個典型的業務，什麼都不懂，就只會出張嘴。

⑦ tremendous：巨大的

We faced tremendous resistance from many user department heads when we tried to implement the ERP system.

在我們試圖實施 ERP 系統時，面臨了許多使用單位主管的強大阻力。

⑧ pressure：壓力

Now that we are designed-in successfully, the pressure turns to the sales team.

既然我們已通過設計承認，壓力就移轉到業務團隊了。

⑨ aspect：方面

I'm confident that we're better than Elba in all aspects.

我有信心我們在每一方面都比 Elba 好。

⑩ resource, cost, quality, schedule, satisfaction, and scope：**PM** 六大評量指標：資源、成本、品質、時程、滿意度、範圍。

⑪ be held responsible：要對…負責

Jeffrey will be held responsible for the successful implementation of the 6 Sigma program.

Jeffrey 將要對成功實施 6 Sigma 負責。

⑫ launch：發射、上市、提出

Because of the incident, the product launch has been pushed back indefinitely.

由於那事件，產品上市時間被無限期延後。

⑬ overall performance：整體績效

In spite of the increased system downtime, the overall quality performance of Q3 and Q4 was satisfactory.

儘管系統故障時間增加，第三、第四季的整體品質績效依舊讓人滿意。

⑭ partner：夥伴

To ensure a strong value chain, we worked closely with all our business partners.

我們和所有生意夥伴密切合作，以確保一條強而有力的價值鏈。

⑮ co-workers：同事（所有工作夥伴泛稱）

Susan gets along with her co-workers.

Susan 和同事們相處很融洽。

NOTE

⑯ **as a consequence**：因此

There was an error in the final stage of the sample preparing. As a consequence, we were forced to put off the launch.

我們在樣品製作最後階段出了一點差錯。因此，我們被迫延期推出。

⑰ **day-to-day**：每天的、日常的

The blackout didn't affect our day-to-day operations.

停電並沒影響我們日常作業。

⑱ **co-ordination**：協調

Co-ordination is what a project manager does all day long.

協調是專案經理從早到晚都在做的事情。

⑲ **take up**：佔據

Meetings take up more than 90% of my working hours in the office.

開會佔掉我九成以上在辦公室的工作時間。

⑳ **majority**：大多數、大部分

The majority of the sales reps prefer a base-income plus incentive package.

大多數業務代表比較喜歡固定收入加激勵獎金的待遇配套。

21 reward：獲得獎賞、報酬

All my 3-year hard work was rewarded when I saw my books in print.

看到我的書上市販售，3 年來的辛苦都值得了。

22 by contrast：相形之下、比較起來

By contrast, we are smaller, but better.

相形之下，我們比較小，但是比較好。

23 collaborate：協同

In order to create higher customer value, we have to make sure that ERP, SCM, and CRM collaborate with each other.

若要提升客戶價值，我們得確保 ERP、SCM、和 CRM 的協同作業。

24 award：（動）給與

We were just awarded an enormous order by Moore Steel.

Moore Steel 方才下了一張大訂單給我們。

25 initiate：發起、啓動、開始

It was Sharon who initiated the study group in the company.

發起公司內部讀書會的是 Sharon。

26 conference call：多方電話會議

Marty, the conference call with Marcom has been delayed to 3:00 p.m..

Marty，和 Marcom 部門的多方電話會議已延到下午三點了。

NOTE

㉗urgent：緊急的、急迫的

We've just received an urgent request from Mason Automation for on-site calibration service.

我們剛剛收到 Mason Automation 要我們提供現場校正服務的緊急要求。

㉘anxiety：焦慮、不安

The project audit caused a great deal of anxiety to the team.

專案稽核帶給團隊極大的焦慮。

㉙samples：樣品、樣機

Bruce, we need to send the samples to Axiom Automation today.

Bruce，我們今天得寄樣機給 Axiom Automation。

㉚speed up：加快、加速

Randy, you need to speed up developing new crystal vendors.

Randy，你得加速開發新的石英震盪器供應商。

㉛press：（動）催促、加壓

Chris, please don't make me have to press you. You must deliver on time.

Chris，請別逼得我來催，你必須得準時交貨。

㉜push：催促、逼迫

Ella, please push Max to submit the monthly quality report no later than 11:00 this morning.

Ella，請催 Max 在今早 11:00 之前交品質月報。

33 **pushing me real hard**：催我催得很緊

34 **I've done all I can**：我已盡全力去做

也可說 I've done as much as I can.

I'm sorry about the delay, Karen. I've done all I can.

Karen，對於延誤我感到很抱歉，我已經盡全力去做了。

35 **how much time it takes**：得花多少時間，動詞用 **take**。

Benny, how much time does it take to complete a temperature testing cycle?

Benny，做完一次溫度測試週期要花多少時間？

36 **shorten**：縮短

Vicky, we'll have to shorten the lead time ASAP.

Vicky，我們得儘快縮短交期。

37 **appreciate it**：謝謝你

非常口語的說法，多在平輩或很熟識的朋友之間使用。

Tom, here's the book that you were looking for.

Tom，這是你在找的那本書。

Appreciate it, Bob.

謝謝你，Bob。

NOTE

㊳ BOM：料表

Bills of Materials 的縮寫。

Billy, when will the BOM of Project Wolf be ready?

Billy，Wolf 專案的料表何時能完成？

㊴ audit：稽核、查帳

Alfred, do you know that the headquarters are going to audit our projects next week?

Alfred，你知道總公司下星期要來稽核我們的專案嗎？

㊵ finalize：完成、定案

Jake, when will you be able to finalize your trip plan?

Jake，你的出差計畫什麼時候才能定案？

㊶ schedule：（動）排定

Sandy, a meeting has been scheduled at 2:00 p.m. Friday afternoon, with the design team.

Sandy，和設計團隊的會議已經排在星期五下午兩點。

㊷ look to：希望、期望

I'm looking to meet you guys in two hours from now.

我期望在二小時後和大家會面。

㊸ depart：離開

Greg's going to depart at 8:00 tonight.

Greg 將在今晚 8:00 離開。

㊹ suit：（動）適合、相配

Manny, the style of your presentation does not suit tomorrow's formal technical conference.

Manny，你簡報的風格和明天的正式技術大會不搭調。

㊺ checked into：檢查、調查、核對

Stan, I'll check into our inventory to see if we have what you need in stock.

Stan，我會去查庫存，看看有沒有你要的現貨。

㊻ join：（動）加入

Patti, will you join us to visit some customers next week?

Patti，下週你能和我們一起去拜訪幾家客戶嗎？。

㊼ how's it going?：你好嗎？

一種非常口語的打招呼問好方式。

㊽ it could've been worse：還不錯、過得去

一種非常口語的回答方式。

Hi Nathan, how's it going?

嗨 Nathan，你好嗎？

Hi Andy, it could've been worse.

嗨 Andy，還不錯啊！。

NOTE

㊾under tremendous pressure：在巨大壓力之下、承受很大壓力

In order to be certified by ISO/TS 16949, our QA team has been under tremendous pressure.

為了要取得 ISO/TS 16949 認證，我們品保團隊承受了極大壓力。

㊿turn out to be：變成、成為

Mia's presentation turned out to be a success.

Mia 的簡報非常成功。

51 a couple of：幾個、二個

Speaking of competition, there are a couple of strong competitors in Europe and the U.S.A..

提起競爭，在歐洲和美國有幾家強勁競爭對手。

I'm sorry, Rex. I still need a couple of hours to finish the calibration.

對不起，Rex。我還需要二小時才能完成校正。

52 mishap：不幸事故、霉運

We suffered badly last year as a result of several mishaps.

幾件不幸事故讓我們去年損失慘重。

53 post-mortem：案後檢討會

Team, we will have a post-mortem for Project Pluto next Monday afternoon.

各位，下週一下午我們開 Pluto 的案後檢討會。

54 **hand it over to**：交給、轉給

Helen, about Project Venus, I'll hand it over to you as quickly as possible.

Helen，關於 Venus 專案，我會儘快轉給你。

55 **vacation**：假期

Roger, what's your plan for your summer vacation?

Roger，你暑假有何計畫？

56 **RF Module**：射頻模組

57 **shortly**：立刻、不久、簡短地

Emma headed for the airport shortly after coming out of the steering committee meeting.

Emma 開完策略委員會議不久之後又趕往機場了。

58 **split**：分配

Dora, I'll be sending you the blanket order for Q1 and Q2 with splits by models and by months in an hour.

Dora，我會在一小時內傳 Q1 和 Q2 按型號按月份的長單給你。

59 **through**：經由、通過

Through the online technical service, we helped Atop's technicians successfully calibrate the tank system.

藉由線上技術服務，我們幫助 Atop 的技師們成功完成了桶槽系統校正。

NOTE

⑥⓪ **sit back**：放輕鬆

Upon finishing the calibration, we could finally sit back and eat our late dinner.

一等到完成校正，我們終於可以輕鬆享用很晚的晚餐。

⑥① **cheers**：敬你、乾杯

Cheers, to your health!

祝你健康，乾杯！。

⑥② **hold on**：等一下、別掛斷（通話時）

Hold on, George. Please go back to the previous slide.

等等 George，請你回到前一張投影片。

Hold on please. I'll put you through to Steve.

請別掛，我把電話轉給 Steve。

⑥③ **RFP**：提案要求書

Allen, when will we start reviewing Canter's RFP together?

Allen，我們何時要一起看看 Canter 的提案要求書？。

⑥④ **the second half of the year**：下半年

Richard, I believe we'll catch up fully in the second half of the year.

Richard，我相信我們在下半年會完全趕上進度。

⑥⑤ **didn't even … until**：不…直到

Jerry, you didn't even leave your seat until you heard the news.

Jerry，直到聽到這消息以前，你甚至不曾離開座位一步。

66 upcoming：即將到來的

Cindy prepared a 50-slide presentation for the upcoming global sales conference.

為了即將到來的全球業務會議，Cindy 準備了一份 50 張投影片的簡報。

67 performance review：業績檢討

Every one of us feels a bit nervous about the upcoming performance review.

我們每個人對於即將到來的業績檢討感到有些緊張。

Page
Note

Lesson 6 研發策略

All about roadmaps

課文重點① Summary 1

In compliance with the speedy evolutionary pace of the semiconductor industry, the R&D of electronic products, and consumer electronics in particular, has been closely following the trend of miniaturization, lower power consumption, and better performance. It is one of the major responsibilities of B2B salespeople to keep themselves up to date with the technology roadmap and the new product roadmap. In addition, as a topic of communications, salespeople should regularly keep their customer's buying center informed of the roadmap in order to get access to their customer's new business as early as possible. As we all know, the new product roadmap is one of the two main focuses of B2B industrial marketing alongside customer relationships. It is extremely important for the salespeople to gain more professionalism in this regard.

由於當今半導體技術快速演進，對許多電子產品生產廠家來說，微型化、超省電、高效能成為產品研發的主軸。B2B 業務人員對於產業技術發展與新產品設計開發的關聯性也必須要有通盤的認識。在實務上，作為一種溝通手段，B2B 業務人員可利用新客戶或潛在客戶相關人員來訪（或主動邀約來訪）機會，針對自家公司技術藍圖、新產品開發藍圖做較詳盡說明，也讓客戶能就近在廠區親身感受到公司的技術實力。技術藍圖或新產品開發藍圖和客戶關係是 B2B 工業行銷聚焦所在，也是 B2B 工業行銷業務人員充實自身專業能力最重要的議題，業務人員必須力求精進。

技術／產品藍圖 Technology / Product Roadmap 6-1

Mason：**VP Sales, Alba Technologies (Taiwan)** 業務副總

Emily：**Senior Project Manager, Wonders Ltd. (Singapore)** 資深 **PM**

Emily is visiting Emily 前來拜訪

Mason：Hi Emily, I hope you like what we've arranged for you so far. Now we're going to show you what our product roadmap looks like.

嗨 Emily，希望你還滿意至今我們安排的參觀。現在我們要向你說明產品藍圖。

Emily：It has been very impressive so far. I like it very much. And thank you for arranging all these presentations. Everything has met our expectation, and I believe the technology roadmap will be interesting too.

到目前為止，一切都讓我印象深刻，我很喜歡。謝謝你的安排，所有項目都符合我們預期，我相信這技術藍圖也一定會很有趣。

Mason：Good! From this graph, we can see there are three types of frequency control devices on our new product roadmap for the coming 18 months. We have already completed the kick-off meetings with our clients.

太好了！我們從這個圖裡可看見，在未來 18 個月當中，我們有三種頻率控制元件產品在開發，而且都已經和客戶開完啟動會議了。

Emily：I see. So it seems that miniaturization, lower power consumption and higher frequency are the key tasks of your R&D work. I realized that it is a common designing path that almost all electronic products are following.

我明白了。看來，微型化、低耗電、和高頻，是未來你們研發的主軸。我知道幾乎所有電子產品都遵循這條設計路徑在走。

Mason：Yes, you're correct. Such technology evolutions are driven by the market requirement for the newest consumer electronics, and I believe that you know it equally or better.

完全正確。這樣的技術演進，其實是被市場對於最新消費性電子產品需求所驅動，你一定和我們同樣了解這點，或許還更了解呢。

Emily：Well, it is indeed the trend. We have to pack so many precision components into such a small enclosure, and guarantee the performance.

這個嘛，的確，那是個趨勢。我們得在這麼小的產品外殼裡，塞進這麼多樣精密元件，還得保證產品的特性表現。

Mason：That's very tough. You can clearly tell from these graphs that the packaging size has been shrinking significantly since 6 years ago, from the much bigger size to the present tiny size. And it will be even tinier in 18 months from now.

那真的很難，你從這幾張圖就能了解。從 6 年前開始，封裝尺寸就很明顯的逐年在縮小，從當時還有這麼大，到現在這麼小。到 18 個月後，尺寸還會變得更小。

Emily：That's amazing. I had very little knowledge about crystal oscillators until now, and I am surprised by what you've just shown me.

真的很神奇。之前我對振盪器幾乎完全不了解，剛才我看到的讓我大吃一驚。

：Please also take a look at the maximum frequency of all these items. It increased from less than 50MHz to almost 1GHz in the same timespan.

也請你看看這些產品的最高頻率，在同一段時間裡，從不到 50MHz，增加到將近 1GHz。

：What I can say is that the market requirements for all the new electronic devices have been changing so vastly and quickly in the last five years. New products must be smaller in size, faster in speed, lower in power consumption, and lower in costs.

我能說的就是在過去五年裡，對於所有新電子產品的市場需求一直在快速大幅改變中。所有新產品必須有更小的外觀尺寸，速度要更快，也得更省電，而且成本要更低。

：I couldn't agree more, and thanks for sharing.

再同意不過了，謝謝你的分享。

NOTE

❶roadmap：路徑圖、藍圖，科技產業常用，多指技術藍圖或新產品開發藍圖。

Matt, be sure to prepare well for the coming new product roadmap meeting next Monday.

Matt，請務必準備妥當，以便參加下週一的新產品開發藍圖會議。

❷in compliance with：遵照、與一致

Steve, have we corrected all the non-conformities in compliance with the ISO 9001 rules?

Steve，我們已經遵照 ISO 9001 規定將所有的缺失更正過來了嗎？

❸speedy：快速的、迅速的。

Each of us on the team wish Sandra a speedy recovery.

我們團隊每個人都祝福 Sandra 快快康復。

❹evolutionary：演進的、進化的

The size of a smartphone's processor in recent years has shown a non-linear evolutionary path.

近幾年來，智慧型手機處理器的尺寸呈現出非線性演進路徑。

❺pace：步調

Michael, I want to remind you that the development pace of Project Jupiter has been way too slow.

Michael，我得提醒你，Jupiter 專案的開發步調實在太慢了。

❻ consumer electronics：消費性電子

We gained a nice share in the network communications segment, but did poorly in consumer electronics.

我們在網通區塊市佔率斬獲不少，但是在消費性電子區塊中表現不佳。

❼ in particular：尤其是、特別是

What's the matter with our sales team? We're shrinking in all three tiers, tier one in particular.

我們業務團隊到底在搞什麼鬼？在全部三階區塊裡都萎縮，尤其是在第一階區塊裡萎縮更嚴重。

❽ closely：緊密地、密切地

Frank, no worries. We'll closely watch what our competitors are doing.

Frank，別擔心，我們會密切注意競爭對手的一舉一動。

❾ trend：趨勢

On-time delivery has been a trend in the consumer electronics industry.

在消費性電子產業哩，準時交貨已是個趨勢了。

❿ miniaturization：微型化

Miniaturization has been the focal point of our R&D projects in recent years.

微型化是近幾年來我們研發專案的焦點。

NOTE

⓫ **consumption**：消耗、消費

Diana, you need to reduce the stationery consumption of your department.

Diana，你得減少你部門的文具消耗。

⓬ **performance**：業績表現

Winnie's performance over the last two months has been superb.

在過去二個月中，Winnie 的業績表現極為出色。

⓭ **keep someone up to date**：讓某人得到最新的資訊、讓某人了解最新的狀況

You go ahead and stay with your family for the holidays. I'll keep you up to date through email.

你去和家人度假吧！我會用 email 讓你了解最新的狀況。

⓮ **in addition**：除了之外、另外

In addition, we need to pay a visit to our distributor in France.

另外，我們得去拜訪法國的代理商。

⓯ **topic**：題目、標題、議題

Lisa, will cost reduction be one of the topics of the review meeting tomorrow morning?

Lisa，明天早上的檢討會裡，降低成本會是議題之一嗎？

⑯ **regularly**：規律地、有規則地

Bob, we need to regularly check the accuracy of our testing machines and instruments.

Bob，我們得定期檢查測試機台和儀表的精度。

⑰ **keep someone informed of**：讓某人得到最新的資訊、讓某人了解最新的狀況

等同 keep someone up to date。

Alyssa, please keep me informed of the progress while I'm on the road.

Alyssa，當我出差在外時，請讓我了解最新的進展。

⑱ **buying center**：採購中心

註：B2B 模式中，買方採購中心多半指所有參與採購決策成員所形成的集合體，並不是買方的正式組織。

Mark, we need to establish a solid relationship with each and every one at Dillon's buying center.

Mark，我們得和 Dillon 的採購中心裡每位成員都建立起穩固的關係。

⑲ **get access to**：獲得

We'd better find a more economical way to get access to the resources we need for our higher-end R&D projects.

我們最好為更高階研發專案找出較經濟取得資源的方法。

NOTE

⑳ as we all know：正如我們所了解的

As we all know, temperature testing is the only bottleneck along our production line.

正如我們所知，溫度測試是我們產線中唯一的瓶頸。

㉑ focus：（名）焦點、聚焦

Cindy, the focus of the upcoming sales review meeting should be on the tier one accounts.

Cindy，即將到來的業務檢討會議焦點應該放在第一階客戶身上。

㉒ extremely：極端地、非常地

Barry, please bear in mind that we have an extremely tight timeline for this project.

Barry，請記住，我們這專案的時程非常緊張。

㉓ professionalism：專業特質

Professionalism is one of the most important attributes for a material sourcing personnel.

專業特質是一位物料蒐尋人員最重要的屬性之一。

㉔ in this regard：在這方面

Fiona, you have to be extremely cautious in this regard.

Fiona，你在這方面必須非常謹慎。

㉕ look like：看似、看起來、外觀像

It looks like Jim's team is going to make the deadline.

看起來 Jim 的團隊將趕上最後期限。

㉖ impressive：讓人印象深刻的

Being the least senior member on the team, Josh's performance was quite impressive.

身為最資淺的團隊成員，Josh 的表現令人印象深刻。

㉗ meet our expectation：達到我們的預期

Performance-wise, sorry Michael, you failed to meet our expectation.

就業績來說，抱歉 Michael，你沒能達到我們的預期。

㉘ frequency control device：頻率控制裝置

A tuning fork crystal is a special kind of frequency control device.

音叉式石英震盪子是一種特殊的頻率控制裝置。

㉙ kick-off meeting：啟動會議、專案啟動會議

Sandy, when will the kick-off meeting with Benson Systems be held?

Sandy，我們和 Benson Systems 的啟動會議定在何時？

㉚ it seems that：似乎，看似

Jeremy, it seems that we're lagging behind.

Jeremy，我們進度似乎落後了。

NOTE

㉛ key：關鍵的、主要的

We fabricate all the key components in-house.

我們所有關鍵零組件都是自製的。

㉜ task：任務

Ian, your only task during the period is to raise our productivity by 30%.

Ian，這段期間裡你唯一的任務，就是把生產力提高三成。

㉝ realize：理解、明白、意識到

Denise, I realize that you've done your best already.

Denise，我了解你已經盡力了。

㉞ path：路徑

Monica, we need to find out the critical path for Project Alston.

Monica，我們得找出 Alston 專案的關鍵路徑。

㉟ evolution：演進、進化

The technology evolution of the semiconductor industry in the last five years has been astonishing.

過去 5 年來半導體技術演進實在驚人。

36 **driven**：被驅動

Mike, as an engineer, I don't really like the KPIs by which we'll be evaluated. You must realize that R&D work isn't really driven by these KPIs.

Mike，身為工程師，我真的不喜歡公司用 KPI 來評量我的績效。你一定了解，研發工作並不真的是由這些 KPI 所驅動的。

37 **indeed**：確實、的確、真正的

A friend in need is a friend indeed.

雪中送炭才算真朋友，患難見真情的意思。

38 **pack**：（動）裝入、塞進

It's amazing to see that you engineers have successfully packed so many components on a tiny PCB like this.

看到你們工程師成功將這麼多零組件塞到這麼一小塊印刷電路板上，真的令人驚奇。

39 **enclosure**：外殼

Patrick, we need a stainless steel enclosure for this outdoor application.

Patrick，針對這室外應用場合，我們得用一個不銹鋼外殼。

40 **guarantee**：保證、擔保

Phoebe, I guarantee that my report will be ready tomorrow morning.

Phoebe，我保證明天早上就會把報告完成。

NOTE

41 **tough**：困難的、難搞的、頑強的

Alex, is Debby Johnson, the purchasing manager of Alston, tough to deal?

Alex，Alston 的採購經理 Debby Johnson 很難打交道嗎？

42 **tell**：分辨、辨別、知道

Billy, you stayed up late again last night, didn't you? I can tell from your red eyes.

Billy，你昨晚又熬夜了，沒有嗎？我從你血紅雙眼就知道了。

43 **packaging**：封裝

Pinnacle Inc. is responsible for the packaging of our chips.

Pinnacle 公司負責我們晶片的封裝工作。

44 **shrink**：收縮、萎縮

Look Janet, the rubber tube started shrinking.

Janet 你看，那橡膠套管開始收縮了。

45 **tiny**：微小的、極小的

Nathan, don't underestimate the power of that tiny motor.

Nathan，不要低估那小馬達的威力。

46 **even**：甚至、都…還

Jason, how can you say so, since we don't even know each other.

Jason，你我都還不認識，你怎能如此說啊？

47 **tinier**：更小的，為 **tiny** 的比較級。

48 **amazing**：神奇的、令人驚異的

It's just amazing to see how this small machine works in the manufacturing system.

看到這小小機器在製造系統內的運作，真是令人驚呀！

49 **little**：小、少

I'm sorry Chris. I know very little about pressure sensors.

抱歉 Chris，我不懂壓力感應器。

50 **crystal oscillator**：石英震盪器

51 **take a look**：看一下、瞧一眼

Emma, would you please take a look at my monthly report ASAP?

Emma，能請你儘早看一下我的月報好嗎？

52 **timespan**：期間

多指二事件之間的時間。

This is the second case that has happened in a timespan of 10 years.

這是在 10 年之間發生的第二件案例。

53 **vastly**：廣大地、巨大地

We have vastly expanded our share in the tier one market.

我們已在第一階市場內大幅擴張了市佔率。

NOTE

54 couldn't agree more：再同意不過了

Nick, you said hot weather made you feel dizzy? I couldn't agree more.

Nick，你說大熱天讓你頭昏眼花？我再同意不過了。

課文重點② Summary 2

Currently, particularly with the electronics industry, there exists a procedural mechanism for the system manufacturers to qualify and select vendors for parts and components. Component manufacturers have to go through a procedure of second Source – AVL – BOM (design-in) in order to be officially certified by the buyer. Thereafter, the sales team of the certified vendor will have to work with the purchasers for business allocation and orders. The entire process requires both R&D engineers and salespeople to work collaboratively.

目前，不少產業，尤其是電子產業，系統廠商多半根據固定程序審核選用零組件供應商。這些供應商需經過 2nd source（成為第二供貨來源）– AVL（放上認證供應商名單）– BOM（放入料表 design in）的手續。之後，認證供應商的業務團隊還得與系統廠商採購協商訂單配額與下單。整個過程都需要供應商研發工程師與業務人員的協同作業才能成功。

打入供應鏈 second source/AVL/design-in

Elena：**Sales Manager, X-Link Inc. (Taiwan)** 業務經理

Alex：**Chief PM, Powell Electronics (Singapore) PM** 總監

Elena is visiting Elena 前來拜訪

Alex：So glad to see you again, Elena. Thanks for making a trip to Powell. Quite a number of projects have emerged and it's better that we discuss them face to face. As usual, we'll have to solve some procedural problems such as type approvals and technical design-in.

好高興又見面了，Elena。謝謝你能來 Powell。我們多出了好幾個案子，我想見面談會比較好。照往例，我們得解決程序上的問題，像是型式認證和設計承認。

有機會談新專案，見面討論比較能深入問題。

Elena：Thanks very much, Alex. Yes, there are lots of things on which we need to collaborate. I guess the most important thing is to be certified by you for the projects.

真是謝謝你，Alex。沒錯，好多事情得靠我們協同解決。我想最重要的一件事就是通過你們認證成為專案合格供應商。

要促成生意，買賣雙方必須協同作業，首要工作是依規定拿到認證。

Alex：Yes, to be certified by us is definitely required. It has been one of our supply chain strategies for many years. Let's waste no time and start with the second source qualification.

是的。通過我們的驗證是絕對必要的，那是我們多年來的一項供應鏈策略。不浪費時間，我們就從取得第二供應商資格開始吧！

而認證第一步則是取得第二供貨廠商身分。

Elena：Oh, I'm very familiar with this. We have to meet all of your requirements of the business terms such as capacity and pricing on one hand, and the technical terms on the other.

啊，這我很熟悉，一方面我們得符合你們對商業條件的需求，例如產能和價格。另一方面也得符合你們對技術條件的要求。

Alex：Basically you're right, but in reality it is far more complicated than you might imagine. You know the engineers. Sometimes, they are just too stubborn.

基本上是如此沒錯，不過實際上要比你想像的複雜多了。工程師你是知道的，有時候他們真的固執過頭了。

看起來似乎不難，實際情形卻不盡然，主要原因是涉及額外的工作。

Elena：They certainly are. Many of our engineers acted the same way. But that's why they are engineers. I remember for some of your projects, I was told by you to modify some of the key specs in order to become qualified. To me, it was a great opportunity.

確實如此，我們公司很多工程師也是這樣。不過，那也是他們之所以是工程師的原因吧！我還記得有幾個你們的案子，你告訴我得修改幾項重要規格才能符合要求。對我來講，那是天賜良機啊！

不同職責，想法不同，可以理解。

Alex：Yeah, I know, but it would have been a horrible nightmare for them. I fully understand how you feel.

是啊，我知道。對工程師來說，那會是場噩夢。我完全理解你的感受。

PM 和業務往往有類似的遭遇，都得與工程師溝通協調。

Elena：Very often, the process went back and forth for several rounds before they were finally convinced.

而且這過程經常會來回好幾次，直到他們終於被說服為止。

說服工程師費神費時。

Alex：We've been through this approval process for several projects so far, unfortunately with little success. I really hope it turns out fine this time.

至今為止，我們已經一起經歷過好幾個專案認證過程，很不幸的卻都沒成功。我真希望這次能有好結果。

Elena：I couldn't agree more and we'll surely try our utmost to make it happen.

我再同意不過了，我們一定會盡最大努力達成合作願望。

Alex：The next step is to be listed on our AVL, the Approved Vendor List.

下一步驟就是進入我們的 AVL，也就是放進認證供應商名單。

Elena：I know being on the AVL only gives us a chance to compete with the existing vendors, if we obtain the final approval in time.

我了解進入 AVL 也只代表如果能即時通過認證，我們就有機會和現有供應商競爭。

AVL 只是敲門磚，還得經過層層測試。

Alex：By being approved or certified, we mean your product is being officially included in our BOM. To any supplier like you, it's very tough, I know. A lot of negotiations and compromises took place here, as it takes a ton of our engineering effort to do the extra work during the design-in stage.

所謂產品已被認證或承認，代表該產品已經正式被放進我公司料表 BOM 上了。我了解，對於像貴公司這樣的供應商，拿到認證確實很難。認證過程中，會有許多協商和妥協，為了供應廠商的 design-in 設計承認，我們得投入很多的工程時間和資源去做額外的工作。

直到正式被納入買方料表（BOM）才算正式獲得認可，期間雙方都需下工夫。

Elena：I realize most of our previous cases failed to meet your requirement at this stage.

我知道先前多數的案子，我們都沒法滿足你們這階段的要求。

Alex：Yes, as a new supplier candidate, you will have to submit whatever samples we may need, for all types of tests. Your co-operation is extremely important.

是的，一個新候選供應商必須提送我們所要的測試樣品，你們的配合度就格外重要了。

這階段裡，業務配合送樣做測試爲關鍵所在。

Elena：This is exactly why I need to receive support from our R&D engineers. They have to consecutively stay up late for several weeks to prepare all the samples for testing.

這也正是為什麼我必須得到我家研發工程師支援的原因，他們得連續熬夜加班好幾星期準備好所有的測試樣品。

賣方研發工程師必須全力支援業務製做樣品。

Alex：Once the samples have passed all the tests, your product will be officially listed on our BOM as a certified part or component.

一旦樣品通過測試，你們的產品就會被正式放入我們 BOM 表裡，成為通過認證的零組件。

樣品通過測試，就有資格被正式編入 BOM 而被選用。

Elena：And only then can we say that we have a successful design-in case. It may take as long as six months after being qualified as a second source vendor.

唯有這時才能說我們成功獲得設計承認 design in 了。從被認可成為潛在供應商到 design in，可能需要長達半年的時間。

Alex：Right, a design-in case means an official chance to compete for orders from us. However, you still have to work with our purchasing guys to get the orders.

沒錯，拿到 design-in 代表你們得到正式爭取我們生意的資格，不過你還是得對採購人員下功夫拿到訂單。

拿到 design-in 之後，業務得繼續強化客戶關係，爭取更高的生意配額。

Elena：I understand. It's time a sales guy like me started to do something. But on the engineering end, I want to tell you what our R&D team will be doing and how they are going to assist you on a daily basis.

我明白，這也是我這業務開始幹活的時候了。不過在工程這一邊，我想告訴你我們的研發工程師會如何在日常工作上協助你們。

提供技術或應用支援是一項很有效的競爭利器。

Alex：Wow, that's great. As a matter of fact, this is also something we would seriously consider while we're evaluating suppliers.
哇，太棒了！事實上，這也是我們在評核供應商時會嚴肅考慮的事項。

對客戶來說，技術或應用支援能力確實愈發重要。

Elena：Thanks. Please rest assured that our technical and application support will become very helpful to you in the future.
謝謝你，也請放心，我們的技術和應用支援在未來對你會很有幫助的。

再次強調自己的強項：技術與應用支援能力。

Alex：All we need to do is give you a buzz, right? Trust me, I'll do it as long as I need your support.
我們所要做的，就是打電話給你，對吧？放心，只要有需要你們來支援，我一定會找你的。

客戶當然也期待供應廠商提供全方位服務。

Elena：I'd love to receive your call. However, I'm not saying that our engineers will be with me all the time. Mostly, we'll be able to talk over the phone or by email.

我會很開心你來找我。不過，我家工程師並不一定隨時會和我在一起；多半我們可用電話或電子郵件連絡。

充分利用網路服務平台，提供線上即時服務。

Alex：I found that day in and day out, most of the problems we have with your products were related to the application problems instead of the products per se.

我發現每天下來我們碰到的問題，多屬於應用問題而非產品本身問題。

客戶強調對應用技術的高度依賴。

Elena：I agree with you. To engineers, reading technical specs is as easy as drinking a glass of iced tea in summertime. But when they're connecting our products with your systems, certain bugs popped up unexpectedly. This happens more during the testing and evaluation stage.

這點我同意。對工程師來說，看技術規格就像夏天裡喝冰紅茶那麼簡單。但是一旦把我們的產品接上系統，往往就會出現意想不到的問題，尤其是在測試與評估階段最常發生。

電子零組件與系統電路匹配問題是常見的應用問題。

Alex: You're right, and that was the time our engineers came to me for help, your help though. In turn, this was the time I wanted to touch base with you.

沒錯，到那時候，我們的工程師就會來找我求救，其實是向你們求救啦。反過來，這也是我聯絡你的時機。

問題發生，PM得負責快速解決，凸顯業務與PM關係的重要性。

Elena: Yeah, I understand that. Again, please treat me as your on-site helping hand, and I'll do whatever I can to help you solve problems in time.

是，我了解。再強調一次，請把我當作你們駐點幫手，我會盡一切可能來幫助你們及時解決問題。

結尾業務不忘強調隨時待命的高度配合力。

NOTE

❶currently：目前、當前

Currently, we're not considering adding any new vendors to our AVL.

目前，我們並沒考慮增加任何新供應商到我們認證供應商名單上。

❷exist：存在、有

Paul, dinosaurs no longer exist on this planet.

Paul，在這星球上，恐龍已不存在了。

❸procedural：程序上的

Dan was really mad about all the procedural difficulties he experienced while applying for a new ID.

Dan對於申請新身分證所遇到的諸多程序困難感到非常生氣。

❹mechanism：機制、機構

The mechanism of this tension tester is quite complicated.

這台張力測試機的操作機制很複雜。

❺qualify：使…具有資格、具備合格條件

Alex, in order to qualify for the military business, we need to upgrade our manufacturing facilities.

Alex，要做軍方生意，我們的生產設備就得升級。

❻ **vendor**：供應商

I'm sorry, Jason. Currently we don't intend to expand our vendor base.

抱歉 Jason，目前我們沒打算擴大供應商家數。

❼ **component**：零組件

The passives and the actives are the two main electronic components.

主動元件和被動元件是二種主要的電子零組件。

❽ **go through**：通過、經歷過

After assembly, the products have to go through a strict testing process before being sent for packing.

組裝完成後，產品必須通過嚴格的測試程序後才能送去包裝。

❾ **procedure**：程序、手續、步驟

The only way to get a better result is to follow the procedures.

要得到好結果的唯一方法就是按程序行事。

❿ **second source–AVL–BOM(design-in)**：這裡是指供應商審核評選的步驟：第一步成為第二供貨來源（**second source**）；第二步進入認可供應商名單內（**AVL**）；第三步正是放入料表（**BOM**）中，完成設計承認（**design in**）。

NOTE

⑪certify：證明、驗證

All the parts and components that we used for production were supplied by certified vendors.

我們用來生產的所有配件和零組件都是由認證廠商供應的。

⑫thereafter：從那時以後、之後

Once the technician fixed the power problem, all of the machines ran smoothly thereafter.

在技師解決電力問題之後，所有機台就順利運作了。

⑬allocation：配額、配置、分配

Jim, by now we have fulfilled the allocation previously committed to you by us.

Jim，至今，我們已經把先前承諾給你們的訂單配額履行完畢了。

若要用動詞 allocate：

Paul, let's try to get them to allocate more than half of the business to us, because of our better price and delivery.

Paul，我們有價格和交貨的優勢，來想辦法要他們給我們一半以上的訂單配額吧！

⑭entire：整個的、全部的

Be careful, Frank. One tiny mistake may ruin the entire experiment.

Frank，你得小心。一個小小的差錯就會毀掉整個實驗。

⑮ collaboratively：協同完成地、協力地

Andy's team and Jake's team joined forces and finished the project collaboratively.

Andy 的團隊和 Jake 的團隊同心協力聯手把專案完成了。

⑯ make a trip：安排一趟行程

Nancy, I need to make an urgent trip to Beijing.

Nancy，我得緊急跑一趟北京。

⑰ quite a number of：相當多、許多

Quite a number of questions were brought up by the participants during the Q&A session.

在提問解答時間裡，與會者提出很多問題。

⑱ emerge：浮現、顯現出來

Quality problems have emerged one by one since we changed the supplier.

從我們換了供應商以來，品質問題就一一浮現。

⑲ face to face：面對面地

Bruce, on this issue, we have to talk face to face.

Bruce，我們得面對面來談這件事。

⑳ as usual：照例、照常、如同往常

As usual, Ian didn't submit his report to me until the last minute before the deadline.

一如往常，Ian 又非得拖到截止期限前一分鐘才交報告。

NOTE

㉑ type approval：型式認證

It is essential to get the type approval for the product in order to break into the Indian market.

要想打進印度市場，就必須取得型式認證。

㉒ design-in：設計承認

A successful design-in requires a ton of effort from all the parties involved.

一個成功的設計承認，需要大量來自所有相關單位的努力。

㉓ lots of：很多、許多、大量的

There are lots of tasks still to be completed.

還有很多事情待完成。

㉔ collaborate：協同、協力

Daniel, we've got to collaborate to finish it this time.

Daniel，這回我們必須得協力完成這件事。

㉕ waste no time：立即、抓緊時間

Guys, let's waste no time and get it done now.

各位，抓緊時間，現在就搞定這件事吧！

㉖ qualification：資格、條件

Nathan, your qualifications are perfect for the vacancy.

Nathan，你的條件太適合這空缺了。

㉗ familiar with：對…熟悉

I'm familiar with the certification of ISO/TS 16949.

我對 ISO/TS 16949 認證很熟悉。

㉘ meet somebody's requirement：達到某人的需求

I'm sorry Allen. You failed to meet our requirement for the minimum capacity again.

抱歉了 Allen，你們又無法達到我們對於產能的最低要求。

㉙ business terms：商業條件、交易條件

Jeff, the business terms you proposed last week were rejected by our boss.

Jeff，你上週所提的生意條件被我們老闆打回票了。

㉚ capacity：產能

Don't worry Charlie. We've reserved enough capacity for your orders.

Charlie 別擔心，我們預留了足夠產能給你們的訂單。

㉛ on one hand…on the other：一方面…另一方面…

We're developing new manufacturing know-how on one hand, and continuously upgrading the existing systems on the other.

一方面我們正在開發新製造技術，另一方面也持續在更新現有系統。

NOTE

32 in reality：實際上、事實上

The job looks nothing but routine, but it's quite complicated in reality.

這工作看起來像是例行公事，不過實際上還挺複雜的。

33 far more：遠多過、遠大過

置於比較級形容詞之前。

Most millennials are far more adaptive to the digital environment than their parents.

大多數千禧世代遠比他們父母更能適應數位環境。

34 complicated：複雜的

The situation is more complicated now than ever before.

現在的情形要比之前來得更複雜。

35 imagine：想像

It's hard to imagine how it would be to live without electricity.

很難想像沒有電力的日子會是怎樣一個情形。

36 stubborn：固執的、頑固的、倔降的

Eddie is too stubborn to make any compromises.

Eddie 太頑固，從不妥協。

37 act：行為、舉動、表現出

She acted as if nothing had happened.

她表現出若無其事的樣子。

㊳ modify：修改、修正

Emily, please modify your inventory report according to the meeting minutes.

Emily，請你根據會議記錄修改你的存貨報告。

㊴ key specs：關鍵規格

specs 爲 specifications 的簡寫。

As I told you in the meeting, you need to tighten up some of the key specs of your machine.

就如同會議中我說的，你們的機器某些關鍵規格得訂的更緊些。

㊵ horrible：可怕的、恐怖的

The injury to the CNC machine operator looked horrible.

那位 CNC 加工機操作員的傷勢看起來好恐怖。

㊶ nightmare：惡夢、夢魘

Making the annual budget has always been a nightmare for me.

對我來說編製年度預算一直是個夢魇。

㊷ go back and forth：往返、來來回回

Morris went back and forth between Shanghai and Taipei to ensure that everything was in good order.

為了要確保一切都安排妥當，Morris 來回奔波於上海台北兩地。

NOTE

㊸ round：回合

Mia and I bargained for several rounds before we settled at this unit price.

Mia 和我討價還價了好幾回才定下這個單價。

㊹ through：通過、經過、經由

Through our efforts, we regained support from this client.

透過努力，我們重新獲得這家客戶的支持。

㊺ little success：不成功、沒有成功

在此，little 解釋成少到幾乎沒有。

We once tried to penetrate into the tier 3 market, but with little success.

我們一度試圖打進第三階市場，卻沒有成功。

㊻ turn out：發生、產生、結果是

The experiment turned out to be a success.

實驗結果是成功的。

㊼ try our utmost：盡我們最大努力

Emma. I promise you that we'll try our utmost to deliver on time.

Emma，我答應你會盡最大努力準時交貨。

㊽ make it happen：做成功、成功實踐

Now that we have our target in place, let's make it happen!

既然我們的目標已確定，我們一起努力達成吧！

49 **list**：列入、登記。

Coaching is being listed as the top responsibility of a sales manager in our company.

在我們公司，指導下屬業務同事被列為一位業務經理的首要責任。

50 **obtain**：獲得、取得

Ryan just obtained permission from Bob to start the maintenance work on the temperature chambers.

Ryan 剛剛得到 Bob 的允許，開始維護溫控箱。

51 **by … we mean…**：所謂…指的是

By FAE, we mean field application engineer, the engineer who helps the customer to use the company's products correctly and effectively.

所為 FAE，指的是應用工程師，協助客戶正確且有效使用公司產品的工程師。

52 **include**：包含、包括

The manufacturing facilities we purchased last week include both mechanical gears and electronic instruments.

上週我們所採購的製造設備包括機械設備和電子儀器。

53 **negotiation**：協商、商議

At a lengthy meeting this morning, there were numerous rounds of negotiations regarding business co-operation between the two companies.

今早冗長的會議中，兩家公司針對合作案有過無數回的協商。

NOTE

54 compromise：讓步、妥協

Michael, under such circumstances, I suggest that we compromise on the product warranty.

Michael，在這情況下，我建議我們在產品保固上讓步。

55 take place：發生、舉行

The product seminar will take place at three o'clock this afternoon.

產品研討會將在今天下午三點舉行。

56 a ton of：大量、很多

Samantha, you'd better take a break now, as we'll have a ton of work to do tonight.

Samantha，你最好現在先休息一下，因為今晚我們還有很多事要做。

57 previous：先前的、早先的

Amanda, would you please refer to my previous mail regarding this issue?

Amanda，能麻煩你去參考我先前給你關於這議題的電子郵件嗎？

58 fail to：無法、沒能

Tiffany was upset, as she failed to come up with a solution in time.

Tiffany 懊惱沒能及時想出解決方案。

59 **candidate**：候選人

Lisa is one of the candidates for our customer service manager vacancy.

Lisa 是我們客服經理職缺的候選人之一。

60 **submit**：提交、交出

Jason, you were supposed to submit your monthly report by 10:00 this morning.

Jason，你本應該在今早 10 點之前交出你的月報告。

61 **co-operation**：合作

Ella, thanks very much for your co-operation in this regard.

Ella，很感謝你在這方面的合作。

62 **exactly**：正是、精確地、完全地

Linda, that's exactly what I want to say.

Linda，那正是我要說的。

63 **consecutively**：連續地

After working consecutively on the case for weeks, Joan and Mark came up with a creative value proposition.

在連續好幾星期專注在這案子之後，Joan 和 Mark 提出了一個有創意的價值提案。

64 **stay up late**：熬夜、深夜不睡

The entire team stayed up late again figuring out how to solve the problem.

整個團隊再次熬夜設法想出解決方案。

NOTE

65 once：曾經、一度、一旦

Cindy, once the shipment arrives, please send the materials to the production line immediately.

Cindy，一旦到貨，請立即把原料送到生產線。

66 officially：正式地、官方地

The launch date has officially been set for July 23.

上市日期已正式定在 7 月 23 日。

67 part：零件、配件

Patrick, don't forget to bring enough spare parts with you.

Patrick，別忘記隨身帶好足夠的備用零件。

68 only (by now) can we say：直到（現在）我們才能說

Only by now can we say that we solved the problem.

直到現在我們才能說問題解決了。

以 only 開頭的句型，動詞要以倒裝方式置於主詞之前。

Only with your consent will we start working with the damaged machine.

只有得到你的許可，我們才會開始動手修理這台損壞的機器。

69 as long as：只要、如果

Barbara, you may stay as long as you like.

Barbara，你喜歡的話，想待多久就待多久。

NOTE

⑦⓪ **it's time someone started to do**：注意 it's time 後面動詞必須用過去式。

Phil, it's time you finished testing these sensors.

Phil，你該把這些感應器測試完成了吧！

⑦① **on the … end**：在 … 這端

On the manufacturing end, we'll be supported by a team of 5 production engineers.

在製造端，會有 5 位製造工程師提供支援。

⑦② **on a daily basis**：每天、按每天

Team, I'll be monitoring your performance on a daily basis.

各位，我將會每天監看你們的業績表現。

⑦③ **as a matter of fact**：事實上、其實

As a matter of fact, we're ahead of schedule already.

事實上，我們進度已經超前。

⑦④ **evaluate**：評估

Guys, I'll start evaluating your Q2 performance tomorrow.

各位，明天我就要開始評估你們第二季業績。

⑦⑤ **rest assured**：放心

Ruby, please rest assured that we'll get it done later today.

Ruby，請放心，我們今天稍晚就會完成這件事。

NOTE

(76) give someone a buzz：打電話給某人

John, please give me a buzz after you finish the calibration.

John，完成校正後請你打電話給我。

(77) all the time：一直、始終

Rex, you have to stay focused all the time to avoid making mistakes.

Rex，你得一直保持專注以免發生錯誤。

(78) day in and day out：日復一日、每一天

Our R&D engineers have been working on the project, day in and day out.

我們的研發工程師們日復一日不停在進行這專案。

(79) instead of：而不是

Bobby, please try harder to negotiate with Denise, instead of complaining to us.

Bobby，請再努力和 Denise 協商，而不是對我們抱怨。

(80) per se：本身、本質上

The problem lies in our operator, not in the instrument per se.

問題出在我們操作人員身上而不在儀器本身。

(81) technical specs：技術規格

Kenny, please check carefully to make sure the technical specs meet our system requirement.

Kenny，請仔細核對來確認技術規格能符合我們系統需求。

82 bug：錯誤、缺陷

Guys, since this is the beta version, I suspect certain bugs are inevitable.

各位，由於這還只是測試版本，我認為難免會出錯。

83 pop up：跳出、彈出

A variety of error messages popped up during the testing phase.

在測試階段，各種錯誤訊息紛紛跳出。

84 unexpectedly：出乎意料地、沒能料到地

Isabelle recorded an unexpectedly high level of performance in her rookie year as a salesperson.

Isabelle 在業務新手期間留下出乎意料的優秀業績。

85 though：雖然、不過、儘管

Tony, I'm glad that you made it, a bit late though.

Tony，儘管你晚到了些，我還是很高興你趕來了。

86 touch base with：聯繫、聯絡、建立關係

I need to touch base with Emily now for help with this issue.

我現在得聯絡 Emily，請她在這議題上幫忙。

87 helping hand：幫助、援助

Jack, please ask Eddie if we can get a helping hand from him.

Jack，請你去問 Eddie 看看他能否幫我們一把。

Page
Note

新產品開發 New Product Development

課文重點① Summary 1

The core of a B2B business model is composed of two elements, namely buyer-seller relationships and new product development. Both require close collaboration among all functional departments such as R&D, marketing, sales, PM, operations, and finance. R&D engineers directly engaged themselves in developing the technologies, products and processes, whereas the marketing and sales teams researched and provided business intelligence as well as market forecasts to generate the projected financial result. The PM function is to initiate, co-ordinate and monitor the progress of each project, to ensure successful development.

客戶關係及新產品開發是 B2B 商業模式的核心，二者都需要公司內部所有部門如研發、行銷、業務、PM、作業、與財務密切協同作業。研發工程師直接參與技術、產品、與製程的開發；行銷與業務團隊負責各項研究與資訊情報整合，更得做出市場預測以便估算財務結果。PM 則主動負責溝通協調，並且監控每項專案進度以確保開發案順利成功。

業務如何參與開發？ How we contribute?

7-1

Amy : **VP Marketing, Luxent Technologies (Taiwan)** 行銷副總

Roy : **VP Sales, Luxent Technologies (Taiwan)** 業務副總

Michael : **Senior R&D Manager, Sonica Inc. (New Zealand)** 資深研發經理

Michael is visiting and performing a factory audit.

Michael 拜訪並做工廠稽核

Amy : Hi Michael, I'm very glad to have you here today, and we're going to share our new product development plans with you. This is Roy, our VP of Sales. I guessed that you two knew each other already. Roy is also a member of our new product development committee.

嗨 Michael，很高興你今天能來我公司，我們將和你分享新產品開發計劃。這是我們業務副總 Roy，我想你們已經認識了。Roy 也是我們新產品開發委員會成員之一。

Michael : Hi Amy, hi Roy. I'm glad to be here to learn more about your business operations. It will be very interesting to see how you marketing guys engaged yourselves in new product development.

嗨 Amy，嗨 Roy。我也很高興能來深入學習貴公司整體作業。

能實際了解你們行銷人員，是如何參與新產品開發過程一定很有趣。

Amy：Firstly, we're fortunate to have a professional marketing team, especially because most of our marketing people came from R&D or the engineering department. I think that is critical to the success of the tasks we were assigned to. The industry is so technically-oriented that anyone without sufficient technical training will not be able to do the job well.

首先，我們很幸運有專業的行銷團隊，特別是因為絕大多數行銷人員是從研發或工程部門轉任的。我認為這對於達成公司所交付的任務，是一項非常重要的安排。這是一個高度技術導向的產業，任何人如果沒有充分的技術訓練是無法勝任的。

Michael：But how do you constantly get sufficient industry and market information and come up with your own propositions?

但是你們又如何能不斷獲取足夠產業與市場資訊，然後做出產品開發提案？

Amy：I'll give you an example. We attended tradeshows to meet and talk to the customers, and sometimes the competitors. And we also attended industry seminars or webinars. And of course, we work closely with our salespeople, as they're always on the front line. From time to time, we make joint sales calls to our customers too.

我舉一個例子來說明。我們會參展，直接與客戶面對面交談。或許也會和競爭對手碰面交換意見，而且我們還會參加產業研討會或線上研討會。當然，因為業務永遠都在第一線，我們會和他們密切合作，並且不時一起拜訪客戶。

Michael：What do you do with all the information that you get from the market?

那你們是如何運用從市場得來的資訊？

Amy：We have to regularly come up with certain development proposals, based on our technical and marketing analyses.

根據技術和行銷分析，我們得定期提出產品開發提案。

Michael：Very good. Thanks Amy. How about you, Roy? How do you engage in the new product development?

真好，謝謝你，Amy。Roy，你呢？你是如何參與新產品開發的？

Roy：I must say that I've never been a technical guy. However, I have been participating in our new product development activities since I was just a junior sales guy. I think it is the first-hand information that a salesperson obtained from regular meetings with the customers that contributed the most to the development plans.

我得說，我從來不是一個懂技術的人。然而，從我還只是個菜鳥業務開始，我就一直參與新產品開發的工作。我認為身為業務，對於新產品開發最大貢獻，就是從與客戶定期開會討論中，所得到的第一手資訊。

Michael：Roy, I totally agree with you on this.

這點我完全同意。

Roy：We deal with problems, all kinds of problems, almost on an hourly basis. It is extremely important for us to have someone we can go to for certain help, without delays.

我們業務人員得解決問題，各式各樣的問題，而且幾乎時時刻刻都如此。業務在組織內找到能夠及時提供必要支援的團隊，是非常非常重要的。

Michael：And I would say, Roy, you've done a great job, really.
這點 Roy，我必須說，你做的棒極了。

Roy：By interacting closer with your R&D engineers, project managers, and production engineers, I learned a lot.
藉由與你們研發工程師、專案經理、以及製造工程師密切互動，我學到很多。

Michael：So you would prepare your proposals from the sales viewpoint for your new product development meeting?
所以，在你們新產品開發會議中，也會將業務所準備的提案納入討論嗎？

Roy：Yes, we do. And of course, we have to fight with our own people from R&D, PM, and other departments. But in the end anyway, we'll have a good product development plan in front of us.
是的，我們會這樣做。當然，業務得和研發、PM、和其他部門的人打仗。但無論如何，最後我們每人面前都會有一份很棒的產品開發計畫書。

NOTE

❶core：核心、中心

The core concept of new product development is to fulfill a certain target market demand and generate optimal benefit for the company.

新產品開發的核心概念，就是藉由滿足特定目標市場需求而帶給公司最適利益。

❷be composed of：由…組成

The project team is composed of two application engineers and one R&D engineer.

專案團隊是由二位應用工程師和一位研發工程師所組成。

❸element：元素、成分、元件

An alloy steel will contain several different metallic elements.

合金鋼含有多種不同金屬成分。

❹collaboration：協同、協力

The project requires a collaboration of R&D, operations, product management, and sales functions.

這專案需要研發、作業、產品管理、和業務的協同作業。

❺engaged oneself in：從事於、在做

Sandra has been engaging herself in developing a mobile CRM system for the sales department.

Sandra一直在替業務部門開發一套行動版客戶關係管理系統。

❻ **whereas**：而、然而

The engineers successfully fixed the mechanical problems of the sorting station, whereas the human-machine interface constantly broke down.

工程師成功修好了分檢站的機械問題，然而人機介面卻一直故障。

❼ **research**：（動）研究、調查

Daniel, please research the subject of IoT and prepare to deliver a presentation next week.

Daniel，請你去研究物聯網這題目，下週做一次簡報。

❽ **business intelligence**：商業智能、商業智慧

Nowadays, business intelligence has become a lot more important and we use it to build up our competitiveness.

現今，我們用以建立競爭力的商業智慧已經顯得愈發重要。

❾ **generate**：產生

Abby, your performance will be appraised by the contribution you have generated in the past 6 months.

Abby，你的績效將由你在過去半年裡對公司的貢獻來評估。

❿ **project**：（動）計算、估算

The Q3 B/B ratio is being projected to exceed 1.2.

第三季的接單出貨比估計會高於 1.2。

NOTE

⑪ initiate：開啓、開始、發起

Randy, you'd better initiate a dialogue with Lisa at ATP now, concerning their delivery plan for next month.

Randy，關於 ATP 下個月的交貨計畫，你最好現在就開始和 ATP Lisa 聯絡。

⑫ monitor：監控、監視

To ensure a perfect testing result, we will be closely monitoring these instruments, without fail.

為了確保完美的測試結果，我們一定會嚴密監控這些儀器。

⑬ ensure：保證、確保

To ensure that we catch up with the schedule sooner, we've been requested to work overtime for the entire week.

為了確保及早趕上交貨時程，我們被要求整個星期都得加班。

⑭ factory audit：工廠稽核

Patti, you have to conduct a factory audit at Redding Steel ASAP.

Patti，你必須儘快到 Redding Steel 進行一次廠稽。

⑮ I'm very glad to have you here：我很高興你能來，是比較口語的說法。

不然也可說：I'm glad you came to visit us.

⑯ **know each other**：彼此認識

each other 爲彼此的意思。

Alex and I have known each other for more than 20 years.

Alex 和我相識已超過 20 年了。

⑰ **committee**：委員會

⑱ **fortunate**：幸運的

We were fortunate to complete the tough mission in such a short time.

我們很幸運能在這麼短時間內完成這項艱難的使命。

⑲ **professional**：專業的

Eric, to become a professional applications engineer, you have to quickly build up your hands-on expertise.

Eric，若要成為一位專業應用工程師，你得快速建立動手實作的專門技術。

⑳ **critical**：關鍵的、重要的

Susan, on time delivery is so critical to a manufacturer like us.

Susan，對我們這種製造廠商來說，準時交貨實在太重要了。

㉑ **task**：任務、工作

Chris has just been assigned the difficult task of doubling our capacity by the end of the year.

Chris 方才被賦予一項在年底前將產能加倍的高難度任務。

NOTE

㉒ assign：指派、指定、分配

Pete assigned Rex to attend the product seminar to be held next Monday.

Pete 指派 Rex 參加下周一舉行的產品研討會。

㉓ technically-oriented：技術導向的

Monica, I don't think the seminar is going to be interesting, as it is too technically-oriented.

Monica，我不認為那會是一場有趣的研討會，因為太技術導向了。

㉔ sufficient：充足的、足夠的

Allen, you don't seem to have had sufficient sleep.

Allen，你似乎睡眠不足。

㉕ be able to：能夠、有能力

No worries. We will be able to supply all the items you need.

別擔心，我們有能力供應所有你需要的品項。

㉖ constantly：不斷地、經常地、持續地

No problem, Bruce. We'll constantly keep you updated on the progress of the experiment.

沒問題，Bruce。我們會持續不斷讓你了解最新的實驗狀況。

㉗ come up with：提出、想出

Larry managed to come up with a technical white paper for our high accuracy instruments.

Larry 設法提出了我們高精度儀器技術白皮書。

㉘ proposition：提議、建議、主張

Sam's proposition was vetoed by the committee.

Sam 的提議被委員會否決了。

㉙ example：範例、例子

Taking it as an example, I'll show you how we continued to upgrade the performance of our stainless steel products.

我以這個做例子，說明我們是如何持續提升不鏽鋼產品的特性。

㉚ attend：參加

Grace told me that Cindy would attend the conference the next day.

Grace 告訴我 Cindy 會參加隔日舉行的大會。

㉛ tradeshow：展覽、展會

We have two tradeshows included in our budget for the second half of the year.

我們有預算在今年下半年參加兩個展會。

㉜ seminar：研討會

Technical seminars are becoming more important as a promotional tool.

技術研討會正成為一種更重要的推廣工具。

NOTE

㉝ webinar：網路研討會

Thanks to the internet, more and more professionals benefit from attending the webinars.

由於網際網路，越來越多專業人士可以參加線上研討會而受益。

㉞ front line：前線

From time to time, our R&D engineers need to be on the front line with the salespeople, meeting up with the customers.

我們的研發工程師不時得和業務人員一起在第一線與客戶接觸。

㉟ from time to time：有時候、偶而、不時

From time to time, we exchanged harsh words with marketing people in the meeting.

有時候我們在會議 中和行銷人員惡言相向。

㊱ joint sales call：共同業務拜訪

Brian and I will make a joint sales call to Ampex tomorrow morning.

明天上午 Brian 和我會一起拜訪 Ampex。

㊲ regularly：定期地、有規律地

We regularly purge the database to make sure that the ERP system operates in a more efficient way.

我們定期清除資料庫以確保 ERP 系統更有效運作。

㊳ **proposal**：提案、提議

Lillian's proposal regarding reducing overall operating cost was later approved by the CEO.

Lillian 有關降低營運成本的提議稍後獲得執行長批准。

㊴ **analyses**：分析，是 **analysis** 的複數形。

We need more analyses to make the final decision.

我們需要更多分析來做最後決定。

㊵ **how about you?** 那你呢、你如何。

I'm OK, Dave. How about you?

我還不錯 Dave，那你呢？

㊶ **participate**：參加、參與

Fred is going to participate in the welding contest next month.

Fred 下個月要參加焊接競賽。

㊷ **junior sales guy**：菜鳥業務、資淺業務

When I was still a junior sales guy, I listened and watched far more than I spoke.

當我還是個菜鳥業務時，我聽看的機會遠比我開口說的機會高出許多。

㊸ **first-hand information**：第一手資訊

The value of first-hand information is much higher than that of second-hand information.

一手資訊遠比二手資訊來得更有價值。

NOTE

44 contribute：貢獻

We expect our new recruits to contribute to our company from day 1.

我們期待新進人員從報到第一天就開始對公司做出貢獻。

45 the most：最多地

Ian has been backing me up the most, in terms of application engineering.

一直以來，Ian 在應用工程方面給我最多的支持。

46 totally：完全地、徹底地

The schedule of the incoming materials is totally out of control.

進料時程完全失控了。

47 deal with：應付、處理

Customer service staff deal with all kinds of incidents on a 24-7 basis.

客服人員得全天候處理各種事件。

48 on an hourly basis：以小時為基準

Because of the emergency, we're checking the water level on an hourly basis.

由於情況緊急，我們正每小時查看一次水位。

49 extremely：極端地、非常地

Market demand for the ultra-high accuracy instruments has been extremely weak.

市場對超高精度儀器的需求極端疲軟。

50 delay：延後、延誤

Emily, we can't afford any further delay.

我們再也經不起任何延誤。

51 you've done a great job：你已經做得很好了！

Don't be too hard on yourself, because you've done a great job.

別太苛責自己，你已經做得很好了！

52 interact：互動

Wendy, please stay calm when interacting with our potential customers online.

Wendy，在線上與潛在顧客互動時請保持冷靜。

53 viewpoint：觀點、看法

Judging from a viewpoint of finance, I propose we suspend our service in the government sector.

從財務觀點來判斷，我建議中止在政府區塊的服務。

54 in the end：最後、結果、終究

If we continue to fight by undercutting competitors, we'll lose the war in the end.

如果我們持續砍價搶單，終究會輸掉這場戰役。

NOTE

55 **anyway**：無論如何

Kim, you'll have to explain to Nathan first thing tomorrow morning anyway.

Kim，無論如何，你明天早上第一件事就是向 Nathan 解釋。

56 **in front of**：在之前

In front of all his team members, Tim made an announcement that he was leaving the company.

Tim 在他所有團隊成員面前宣布他將離職。

課文重點② Summary 2

The new product development evaluation meeting plays a vital role in the entire new product development cycle. It determines the viability of the technological, marketing, sales, and financial aspects of the development project. Among all these business aspects, the prospect of profitability is usually of the most importance. Only with promising profitability will a development project sustain all the efforts and money it requires to reach maturity. Certainly, prior to analyzing everything else, it is essential to establish that the organization is technically capable of accomplishing the design, the development, and the manufacturing of the new product.

新產品開發過程中，評估會議扮演著極為重要的角色。評估會議的功能在於確認技術可行性、行銷可行性、業務可行性、和財務可行性。其中，未來利潤率展望最重要，唯有可觀的利潤展望，才有著手開發的條件。不過在這之前，有個先決條件，就是企業本身的技術能力有辦法設計出適合生產的新產品才行。

關鍵評估會議 Evaluation - Tech & Finance

Lisa: **VP PM, Luxent Technologies (Taiwan) PM** 副總

Roy: **VP Sales, Luxent Technologies (Taiwan)** 業務副總

Eunice: **VP R&D, Luxent Technologies (Taiwan)** 研發副總

Michael: **Senior R&D Manager, Sonica Inc. (New Zealand)** 資深研發經理

Michael is visiting and performing a factory audit Michael 拜訪並進行工廠稽稽核

Lisa: Michael, I hope you have liked what you've seen so far regarding our new product development planning. In this session , we're going to explain the way in which we manage the development process . This is Eunice, our VP R&D.

Michael，我希望你還喜歡至今所看到的新產品開發計劃。在這段時間裡，我們將會分享開發過程。這位是我們研發副總 Eunice。

Dr. Lee 解析

邀請客戶關鍵人員前來拜訪或稽核是供應廠商在 design in 過程中常見的作法。

Michael：Hi Eunice, very nice to meet you. I enjoyed it very much indeed. It's impressive!

嗨 Eunice，很高興見到你。我非常享受這一切，印象深刻得不得了。

博取好感的良機。

Lisa：Good. Now let's move on. Regardless of the origin of the new project, be it a customer request or an industry trend, an evaluation meeting is required. And it is the most critical meeting, not only for the salespeople, but also for the project managers, as the PMs will be held accountable for the overall performance of the project.

好，我們就繼續吧。無論新開發案的源頭是什麼，來自客戶需求也好，或是產業趨勢也好，我們都得開評估會議。不僅對業務，而且對專案經理來說，評估會議都是最具關鍵性的會議，因為專案經理得對專案整體銷售業績負全責。

評估會議是新產品開發的重頭戲。

Michael：Yes, I understand it very well. We also have a similar system in our company.

沒錯，我很清楚這一點，我們公司情形也很類似。

評估會議幾乎已成產業標準作業。

Lisa：One of the most critical considerations will be the scale of the potential new business, and what the profits will look like if we launch the product as planned.

其中一項最關鍵的考量點，是一旦按照計畫推出，新產品的潛在生意規模以及獲利狀況會如何。

永遠向錢看，商業規模與獲利率都得考慮。

Michael：If it isn't attractive enough, then that's it; no more discussions, correct?

如果不具吸引力，那就結案，根本不必再討論，對吧？

沒商機就別談了。

Roy：Yes, thank you, Michael. Now you know how fragile we salespeople are in this regard.

謝謝你喔，Michael。現在你明白我們業務在這方面是有多脆弱了吧？

一點都沒錯，業務永遠背壓力。

Michael: But I know that marketing also plays an important role at this stage. They have to identify where the exact opportunities are, and do the market forecast accordingly. Am I right?

不過我了解，在這階段，行銷也扮演著很重要的角色。行銷人員得很精確辨識出生意機會在哪裡，並且得做出需求預估，對吧？

當然行銷也得發揮研究分析與預估的功能。

Lisa: Oh my God, you know everything! Roy, why are we still here? I'm just kidding. We'll go into the technical and financial evaluation stage. I would say that this is the most critical part of the entire evaluation process. Would you please, Eunice?

喔，老天，你什麼都知道了！Roy，我們還在這裡做啥？我開玩笑的啦！接下來我們就進入技術和財務評估階段了，我認為這是整個評估過程中最重要的部分。Eunice，麻煩你了。

Dr. Lee 解析

能前來稽核，當然在專業上有深厚功力。技術與財務評估階段更是重頭戲。

Michael: I am looking forward to this session. I'd like to see if we could learn more from you.

很期待來到這階段，我想看看能否向你們多學一些。

Eunice: Well, on the technical side, the most important thing is to make sure we are capable of designing the right product that is viable for manufacturing. So we first run a thorough study of the specs required, and see if we are able to meet all of them, based on all the resources we have internally and externally.

從技術面來看，最重要的是確保我們有足夠能力，設計出能順利生產又符合需要的產品。因此，我們先仔細研究客戶要求的規格，並根據我們公司內外部所有能使用的資源，來衡量我們是否能完全滿足需求。

技術能力當然得考慮公司可用的資源如資金與人力。

Lisa: By then, we are also able to calculate the Capex, capital expenditures, and possibly the ROI of the project.

來到這裡，我們就能一併估算資本支出的規模，連同投資報酬率也可能算得出來。

資本支出和 ROI 是共通語言。

Michael：We do the same in our company. But who will make the final decision?

我們公司作法也相同，但是到底是誰做最後決定？

誰最有決定權？

Lisa：In our system, after the VP of R&D approves, the project will be presented to the CEO, who will then have the final say.

按照我們的系統，在研發副總簽字核准後，開發案會上呈到執行長那兒，由執行長做最後決定。

大老闆才有決定權。

Michael：It makes good sense, particularly if the project would involve heavy capital investment in every aspect. You need to have the approval from the CEO.

如果專案牽涉到多項高額資本投資的話，這樣做很有道理，必需得到執行長的批准才行。

Lisa：However in reality, we dealt a lot more with smaller cases that caused a tremendous tug-of-war between sales and R&D, as well as between sales and finance.

不過實際上我們平常接觸到的多半屬於較小規模的案子，經常得在業務和研發，甚至和財務，之間來回較力。

各部門之間的拉扯在所難免，尤其是業務與研發以及業務與行銷之間的角力。

Michael：I agree. It happens all the time. Again, usually the CEO will have to make the final decision anyway.

我同意，這種情形常常發生。同樣的，通常執行長得做最後裁決。

Dr. Lee 解析

衝突是常態，CEO 還是關鍵。

NOTE

❶ **evaluation**：評估、評核

Team, one-on-one evaluation meetings will begin at 10:00 tomorrow morning.

各位，明早十點開始一對一評核會議。

❷ **play a role**：扮演一個角色

Alex has been playing a crucial role on our FAE team for a long time.

多年來 Alex 一直在我們應用工程團隊中扮演著極為關鍵的角色。

❸ **vital**：絕對必要的、至關重要的

It is vital that we speed up the development immediately.

我們絕對得立即加速開發。

❹ **cycle**：循環、週期

It takes 36 hours to complete a temperature testing cycle.

整個溫度測試週期需要 36 小時。

❺ **determine**：決定、確定

We need more time to determine if we should continue.

我們需要多一些時間來決定是否該繼續。

❻ **viability**：可行性、生存性

Sorry Frank, I don't see any viability with your product concept.

抱歉 Frank，我看不出你的產品概念可行性。

NOTE

❼ **aspect**：方面

We are stronger than our closest competitor in all aspects.

我們在每一方面都比最強競爭對手更強。

❽ **prospect**：展望、前景、期望

The demand prospect of Q3 doesn't look good at all.

第三季的需求展望看來一點都不好。

❾ **of the most importance**：最重要的

The accuracy of the demand forecast is of the most importance to us.

對我們來說，需求預估的精確度是最重要的了。

❿ **only … will**：唯有 … 才

練習以 only 為句首的句型：

Only by committing sufficient capacity to the customers will we be able to constantly win orders from them.

唯有承諾給客戶充分產能，我們才能持續贏得訂單。

Only if we double our capacity will we be able to compete for Morton's business next year.

唯有加倍產能，我們才有辦法爭取 Morton 公司明年的生意。

⓫ **promising**：有希望的、有前途的

The forecast doesn't look very promising.

這預估看起來不太妙。

⑫ **sustain**：支持、支撐、維持

Our operating profits sustain our investment in R&D and manufacturing facilities well.

我們的營運利潤能有效支撐研發和生產設備上的投資。

⑬ **prior to**：在 … 之前、優先於

Prior to the arrival of the new CNC machining center, the engineers had to finish the installation drills.

在心 CNC 加工中心運到之前，工程師們必須完成安裝演練。

⑭ **essential**：必要的

It is essential that all of you show up tomorrow.

你們所有的人明天必須出席。

⑮ **capable of**：能夠、有能力

Relax, Frank. Our engineering team is capable of solving your problems.

放輕鬆，Frank。我們工程團隊有能力解決你們的問題。

⑯ **accomplish**：完成、實現

The engineers worked together for a long time and accomplished the task as expected.

工程師們一起工作了一長段時間後，如期完成任務。

⑰ **session**：會議期間、上課期間、期間

There will be a Q&A session at the end of Allen's presentation.

在 Allen 簡報結束後會有一段提問解答（Q&A）時間。

NOTE

⑱indeed：真實的、真正的、確實的

It is indeed a tough question.

那的確是個很難回答的問題。

⑲impressive：印象深刻的、令人難忘的、很棒很突出的

Ella's R&D achievement is too impressive to forget.

Ella 的研發成就非常突出，想忘記都困難。

⑳move on：繼續、向前

Let's move on. No point in looking back.

繼續往前吧！沒必要回顧從前。

㉑origin：源頭、起源

Instead of pointing fingers, we need to find out the origin of this quality problem.

我們得找出這品質問題根源，而不是互相指責。

㉒be it：不論、不管

When we're trying to figure out a filtering method , be it analog or digital, we have to ensure the overall system accuracy remains within limits.

當我們試著想出一種濾波方式，無論類比或數位，都得確保整機系統精度才行。

㉓ not only … but also：不但 … 而且

Our application engineer not only did the troubleshooting, but also helped the customer do the calibration.

我們應用工程師不但找出故障原因，還幫客戶進行校正。

㉔ held accountable：對 … 負責

Garcia was held accountable for the launch of CTX-75.

Garcia 得對 CTX-75 上市負責。

㉕ overall：整體的、綜合的

Brenda is supervising the overall operations of the factory.

Brenda 督導工廠的整體作業。

㉖ similar：相似、類似

Mike, we're having a similar problem of material shortage as you were 2 weeks ago.

Mike，我們正面臨一個類似二星期前你們所遇到的缺料問題。

㉗ consideration：考慮事項

Julie, capacity is one of the most important considerations while we're evaluating the suppliers to work with.

Julie，當我們在評估供應廠商時，產能是最重要考慮因素之一。

㉘ scale：規模、比例

㉙ potential：潛在的、有潛力的

Oscar is a young mechanical engineer with great potential.

Oscar 是位很有潛力的年輕機械工程師。

NOTE

㉚ launch：上市、推出、發射

The decision was made that we're to launch the new SoC XT8808 by the end of this year.

我們已經決定在年底前推出新系統晶片 XT8808。

㉛ attractive：具吸引力的、有魅力的

It is hard to resist such an attractive job offer.

實在很難抗拒如此有吸引力的工作機會。

㉜ fragile：脆弱的、易碎的

Watch out, Grant. The instrument is too fragile to take any mis-handling.

Grant，當心！這台儀器很脆弱，禁不起任何不當操作。

㉝ stage：階段

Adam, we're in the final stage of the experiment.

Adam，我們正在實驗的最後階段。

㉞ identify：識別、辨認

Susan, would you please identify the defective units among those in the carton?

Susan，能請你從紙箱內貨品中辨認出不良品嗎？

㉟ accordingly：根據、照著、因此

In the end, we had no other choice but to match accordingly.

最後，我們別無他法只能跟價。

36 **kidding**：開玩笑

Never mind, Isabelle. I was just kidding.

沒關係的，Isabelle。我只是在開玩笑。

37 **looking forward to**：期待、盼望

Guys, I look forward to seeing you at the show in Shanghai tomorrow morning.

各位，我期待明天早上在上海展場見到你們。

38 **viable**：可行的、能生存的

Danny, please save your breath, and come up with some truly viable solutions instead.

Danny，省省氣力，你該提出一些真正可行的解決方案。

39 **thorough**：徹底的、全面的、詳盡的

Steve, we must carry out a thorough inspection on our calibration system.

Steve，我們一定得徹底檢查我們的校正系統。

40 **internally**：內部地

Vicky, we have to keep an internally stable organization, in terms of manpower turnover.

Vicky，我們得維持一個內部人員流動率穩定的組織結構。

41 **externally**：外部地

The machining of our sensor elements is being done externally.

我們委外機械加工感應器彈性體。

NOTE

㊷Capex：資本支出

capital expenditure 的縮寫。

In order to support the projected growth of the next three years, we've budgeted more than $2 billion of Capex.

為了維持未來三年的預估成長，我們編列了超過 20 億的資本支出。

㊸ROI：投資報酬率

I'm absolutely sure that the ROI of this project will be greater than 50%.

我有絕對把握本專案的投資報酬率會大於 50%。

㊹make the final decision：做最後決定

Alex, I'll make the final decision later today.

Alex，我今天稍晚會作最後決定。

㊺present：（動）交給、呈現

Jim, I'll present your trip report to Tim tomorrow morning.

Jim，我明早會把你的出差報告交給 Tim。

㊻have the final say：說了算、有決定權

No problem. You all have the right to express yourselves, but I will have the final say.

沒問題，你們有權表達意見，但是我說了才算數。

47 **make good sense**：有道理、有意義

It makes good sense to take a day off, as it has been pouring for hours.

今天放一天假有道理，因為已經下好幾小時大雨了。

48 **involve**：牽涉、涉及

Bruce, the case involves a bona fide third party. I'm going to ask them to participate in our discussion.

Bruce，這案子牽涉善意第三人，我會要求他們參加討論。

49 **capital investment**：資本投資

The capital investment on the new factory will be enormous.

在新廠房上的資本投資金額會非常大。

50 **in reality**：實際上、事實上

In reality, our yield is much higher than we previously expected.

事實上，我們的良率比先前預期高出許多。

51 **tremendous**：巨大的

All of my team members are under tremendous pressure.

所有我的團隊成員都處在極大壓力之下。

52 **tug-of-war**：拔河、角力、激烈競爭

There's always a tug-of-war between sales and marketing.

業務和行銷之間的相互拉扯永遠存在。

NOTE

53 as well as：也、和

The capacity, as well as the price, is a major factor when evaluating suppliers.

如同價格，產能也是評估供應商的一項主要因素。

54 anyway：無論如何

I'll call you to discuss anyway.

無論如何，我會打電話和你討論。

國家圖書館出版品預行編目資料

B2B企業英語會話. 作業研發篇／李純白著.
— 初版. — 臺北市：五南, 2015.12
面； 公分
ISBN 978-957-11-8392-3（平裝）

1.商業英文 2.會話

805.188 104022829

1XOG

B2B企業英語會話～作業研發篇

作 者 — 李純白
發 行 人 — 楊榮川
總 編 輯 — 王翠華
主 編 — 朱曉蘋
封面設計 — 劉好音
出 版 者 — 五南圖書出版股份有限公司
地 址：106台北市大安區和平東路二段339號4樓
電 話：(02)2705-5066 傳 真：(02)2706-6100
網 址：http://www.wunan.com.tw
電子郵件：wunan@wunan.com.tw
劃撥帳號：01068953
戶 名：五南圖書出版股份有限公司
法律顧問 林勝安律師事務所 林勝安律師
出版日期 2015年12月初版一刷
定 價 新臺幣400元

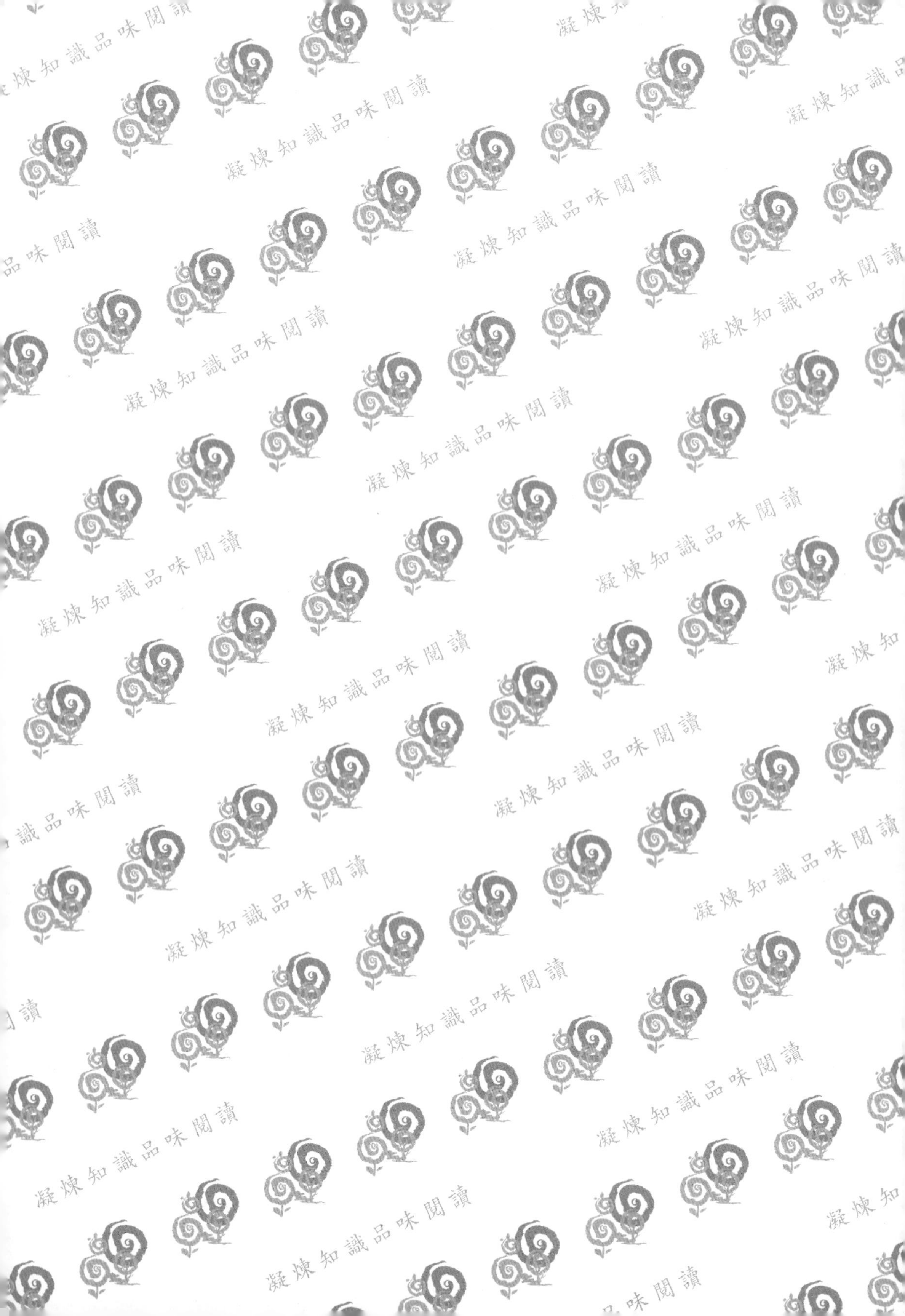